DATE DUE

Demco No. 62-0549

Once on This River

Once on This River

Sharon Dennis Wyeth

Alfred A. Knopf
New York

THIS IS A BORZOI BOOK PUBLISHED BY ALFRED A. KNOPF, INC.

Text copyright © 1998 by Sharon Dennis Wyeth
Jacket illustration © 1998 by Raul Colón

Cover image from the *New York Gazette/Weekly Postboy*, April 9, 1750.
Courtesy of the Rare Books Division of the New York Public Library,
Astor, Lenox and Tilden Foundations.

Source notes for the historical documents that precede each chapter
can be found on page 150.

http://www.randomhouse.com/

Library of Congress Cataloging-in-Publication Data

Wyeth, Sharon Dennis.
Once on this river / by Sharon Dennis Wyeth.
p.   cm.
Summary: While on a trip with her mother from Madagascar to New York in 1760, eleven-
year-old Monday learns the horrors of slavery and the truth about her "other" mother.
ISBN 0-679-88350-9 (trade)
ISBN 0-679-98350-3 (lib. bdg.)
1. Afro-Americans—Juvenile fiction. [1. Afro-Americans—Fiction. 2. Slavery—Fiction.
3. Mothers and daughters—Fiction.] I. Title.
PZ7.W97460n   1998
[Fic]—dc21   97-28779

Printed in the United States of America
10 9 8 7 6 5 4 3 2 1

In memory of the African community of Philipsburg Manor,
offered for auction on April 19, 1750.

Also to the spirit of Martin Colly, the earliest known member of my own
African American family—"a free mulatto with a scar on his face,"
born in 1769.

By A Woman Slave @ #60
By 6 peices bleu & white calocos @ 6p #36
By 3 kettles...#9
By 2 dozen hatts @ 8p...#16

By 2 slaves one boy one garl #84
By 2 kags Powder @ 7...#14

Barted with Capt. John Wades
To Skhds rum 112 gallons @ 3/9 #84
To 70 oynons...#7

By Fish Plantins and Pumkins bought for
slaves at sundary times

By a Boy
By A man #43

From the account book of the sloop *BV Rhode Island*, Peter James, Master, sailed from December 1748 to July 1749.

Chapter One

The baby's feet came first. They were sticking out from the mother. Tiny feet with pale bottoms, the ankles hanging helpless like twigs. Usually the head came first, but tonight the feet were coming, which was the dangerous way of being born. My mother was the midwife. It was my job to hold the torch. The ocean pitched our ship forward. Two sailors stood close by and in the corner of the cabin a huddle of women in thin clothing. The baby's mother screamed. Her skin tore and two tiny legs appeared. One of the sailors, who smelled like rum, cursed in Dutch. The baby's legs hung there. If the rest didn't come out soon, it would smother. Its own mother's body, which had nourished it, had become a monster's mouth. My mother grabbed me by the shoulders and pushed me forward.

"I need your help, Monday. Give him the light."

Mother stationed me in front of her, almost up against the new mother's lap. I thrust the torch toward the Hollander sailor and he took it.

"Be ready to catch, Monday," she said.

I stretched my hands out. I had helped my mother at other birthings, but I had never caught a baby before.

.her pushed the woman's legs apart and leaned into her

_N_!" she screamed.

woman pushed with all her might as the waves tossed our ship u_r ward. Through the soles of my shoes, I hugged the cabin floor. If I had moved an inch from my station, the babe would have been lost. For when my mother had screamed into the woman's face, a dam inside her had broken. The baby was sliding free into my waiting hands! Small dark stomach, chest, arms and shoulders . . . then the neck—wrapped with a pulsing snakelike cord that threatened to hang it! But my mother's deft hand was there also, slipping the snake-like cord from around the small neck just in time for the baby's face and whole head to appear with all the rest that had cushioned it inside of its mother. A girl! I held on to her tightly—the first new life I had caught!

"Good work, Monday," whispered my mother.

The Hollander sailor made a crude hooting sound. I shot him a scowl. What right had he to be present at this sacred moment? I wondered why my mother didn't order him out. Back home in Madagascar, men were not allowed to be present at birthings. I placed the baby on her mother's stomach and my mother tied the cord in two places. Then with a knife she cut it, and the babe took her first breath.

The new mother lifted her head to see and let out a long breath of her own. Nudging me out of the way, my mother swooped the baby up in clean linen and gave it to her. The new mother's face lit up with joy as she looked into the child's eyes. Then the baby let out a hearty cry that filled up the whole cabin. With such a powerful voice, this new life would be a strong one!

• • •

Without warning, the cabin got darker.

"The light!" my mother called out. "Mariner Ten Eyck, leave us the light."

I turned to see the Hollander sailor staggering toward the door. He was taking the torch with him, leaving my mother to complete her business by only the faint starlight that shone through the portal.

"Please leave us the torch, Mariner Ten Eyck!"

"What's left to do, Mistress *Giant?*" the drunken Ten Eyck sang out, making sport of my mother's great height. "I must report to Captain Boyd that a wench is whelped. Then I have to sleep before my watch."

The other sailor stepped out of the shadows. The glare of the torch showed him to be the Spanish one who wore a shell earring. "¡Dámelo!" he said, taking the torch from Ten Eyck. The Hollander opened the door and lurched out into the darkness. "Good work, Leslie de Groot," he muttered over his shoulder in my mother's direction. "This infant might add some value to the cargo, should it survive the voyage to New York." The door banged shut behind Ten Eyck. What strange and hurtful comments the mariner had uttered! Why shouldn't the infant survive, with her mother to take care of her? And what did a baby have to do with the value of the cargo? I turned to my mother. Busy with the afterbirth, she seemed unruffled by Ten Eyck's rude behavior, I suppose because she was used to the ways of mariners. Besides her midwife practice, Mother made sick calls on ships when they came to Madagascar. Since she never took me with her at those times, I had not often been in the company of seamen, except for the master of the *Peggy,* Captain Boyd. Once a year, Captain Boyd rounded the Cape and anchored near the trading post in Ft. Dauphin. He always came to see Mother and me at our house in the village. He would drink Indian tea with us, and play with my lemur. After the visit, Mother would go with him to spend a few days on the *Peggy* to care for the ailing. Seeing to the ailments of mariners passing through was one of the chief ways that Mother earned our living. Long ago, she had even cured Captain Boyd. . . .

Unlike boisterous Ten Eyck, the sailor now holding the torch was completely silent. He had turned his back, which allowed us some sense of privacy. In the corner of the cabin, the group of women in thin clothes began to stir. There were five of them—they came forward into the light to peek at the new baby. They smiled and cooed and one of them stroked the new mother's arm and murmured to her in Kuku, a language spoken by people from Sudan. I knew that, because my best friend at home, whose name is Kiden, came from Sudan and also speaks Kuku. The women began to sing softly. The beautiful tones of their high-pitched voices mingled with the sound of the wind:

Ti Matat purani pura
Ko yungwe na nguro!
Kotumit nikang ako 'dija!
(Praise God
A baby is born!
Let every door be open to her!)

My mother motioned to me to get the bottle of cobwebs she kept in her sack to help stop the new mother's bleeding. When that was done, she cleaned the plank that the new mother was lying on and mopped up all around her. The Sudanese woman who had stroked the new mother's arm helped my mother to clean.

Mother gestured that it was time for us to go. I took one more look at the baby, who was now nursing. Her small head was covered with soft-looking dark fuzz. I longed to hold her again.

"Come along, Monday," my mother said.

The baby's mother looked up at me. The women's singing had stopped. "Monday? . . ."

I leaned in closer. "Yes, I am Monday de Groot," I said, pointing to myself.

With thin, smooth-looking hands, the woman picked up her baby and laid her in my arms. The child's perfect round face was peaceful and her bones were soft as a baby bird's!

The mother murmured my name. "Monday."

The other women smiled at me and began nodding.

"She is naming the baby for you," my mother whispered to me.

"Oh, thank you!" I said, feeling a jolt of pride.

"Now give the child back," Mother murmured.

I let the delicate bundle slip back into its own mother's arms.

Mother bowed and reached for me. The Spanish sailor had opened the door. I bowed also and we left.

We parted ways with the sailor on deck. He took the torch with him. I stumbled forward, tripping on the new British-style skirt I was wearing. Mother had gotten the drab cloth at the trading post in exchange for plantains. That was also the day when she had arranged with Captain Boyd to take us to America in exchange for her services on board. Though Mother had been born in America, she scarcely spoke of it. But for some reason, she had decided that we should go for a visit to her family.

"You caught the baby very well," Mother said. A strong breeze whipped her cloak. "I'm sure it's the mother's custom to name a child for an ancestor. The mother has done you great honor by naming her child Monday."

"Especially since today is Friday!" I exclaimed. I had been called Monday because Monday was the day of the week on which I had been born. "Such a beautiful baby and she's named for me! I hope I know her the rest of my life! Of course, I love all new babies," I gushed. "I suppose I got that from you."

"Just because I sometimes help to bring babies out does not mean that I am overly fond of them," Mother remarked. "The only baby I liked at once was you."

"Of course you liked me. All mothers like their own children."

She put her hand on my shoulder. "Be quiet." We opened the door to our cabin and tiptoed past our sleeping cabin mates, Mr. and Mrs. Kendrickson, a Quaker couple who had come aboard in England. The Kendricksons were going to settle in a place called Lebanon Springs, New York, where other Quakers they knew had a farm.

We lifted the curtain that divided the room and ducked under. Mother lit the lantern, while I set about scrubbing my hands and arms with soap, rinsing in the bucket of salt water we used for such things. Then from our drinking pouch, we each drank a mouthful of the fresh water which is rationed on the ship. On the table in the corner was a bowl of cold rice which I ate with my fingers, along with one of the hard biscuits which had been doled out to the passengers. "Tomorrow I'll mash some plantains and beans to make jumqua for the new mother," I said, almost breaking my teeth on the biscuit. "There is not enough strength for her and little Monday in this hard bread they serve here."

"We have eaten most of the fruit we brought with us," my mother pointed out.

"Captain Boyd will have to give us some," I said.

"I'll ask in the galley. I did see the crew bringing on pumpkins."

"I hope the baby is warm enough," I added. "Why did the women in that cabin bring so little clothing? I'll ask Captain Boyd for an extra blanket."

"It's not your place to speak with him about it," said Mother.

"A new baby needs warmth," I argued.

"I will do what I can," said Mother, "but those people are really the business of Captain Boyd."

"Why are they his business? Do they work for him, like you do?"

Mother sighed and shook her head.

"I wonder whether they are also going to New York," I prattled on. "Come to think of it, I never saw them get on board. I haven't seen them on deck, for that matter."

Mother touched my shoulder gently and sat me down.

"The reason we have not seen the baby's mother and her companions before is that they are confined."

"Why? Because the mother was about to give birth?"

Mother lowered her eyes. "They are a part of the cargo," she said.

"Ten Eyck also said something silly like that. The *Peggy* is carrying muskets and calico, rum and vanilla, and suchlike—Captain Boyd told me at dinner. How can people be part of a cargo?"

"They are slaves," Mother said.

Her words hung in the air. For a moment my breath was taken away.

"You're wrong," I choked. "Captain Boyd said that he is carrying one hundred kettles and seventy muskets for barter."

"And with his kettles and muskets, he also has eleven people. The six Sudanese women came aboard in Rwanda. Boyd got them from

Portuguese traders. The five men are Angolan. I have been below to tend to one of the men, who has a fever. You would not have seen any of them if I hadn't needed you to assist me with the birth."

Tears sprang to my eyes. Though I had had little contact with slavery, I knew that it was something horrible. Once at the trading post, when Mother was buying spices, I had wandered away and caught sight of a group of men pressed back to back, trapped beneath a large net. Their heads drooped and their bodies were thick with flies. I stared in horror, wondering how they had come to such a state. Then one of them caught my eye and asked for water. I hurried forward, but was stopped by one of the locals, a man named Solomon, who usually sold lemurs. He was in the midst of haggling with a European with mangy hair and an eye patch. The thirsty man called out again, seeking my eye through the ropelike cage. Meeting his agonized expression, I began to scream in fright and pity. When she heard my scream, Mother came running to snatch me up and carry me home. Later I asked her what the men had done to deserve such a punishment. She told me that they had done nothing. That they had been stolen from their homes in the north and were going to be sold. Recalling the thin, smooth hands of the mother who had just given birth on our ship and the lusty cry of her baby, I began sobbing.

"They can't be slaves! Captain Boyd has made a mistake."

"The mistake is that anyone at all should be a slave," Mother said, stroking me.

"But the baby has just been born. Her whole life is ahead. No one has the right to take it! I thought that Captain Boyd was kind! But now I hate him!"

"Hush," Mother said, patting my back. "You'll disturb the

Kendricksons." I sat down in the corner, and bit my lip to stifle my crying. Mother spread my pallet on the floor.

"Can't we help Monday and her mother?" I whispered across the room.

Mother shook her head.

"But Captain Boyd is your friend. You can ask him to let them go."

"Captain Boyd is not my friend," Mother said.

"But you saved his life when he had the fever."

"I saved his life because I was paid to," said Mother. "I work for him because I must make a living. He did not always traffic in slaves," she added quietly.

I lay down on the pallet and she covered me with her cloak.

"The women were so happy," I murmured. "How could they be so joyful when their lives have been stolen?"

"The birth of a child brings a heavenly light into the world, which is even more welcome when your life is overtaken by darkness," said Mother.

"What will happen to baby Monday?" I asked, staring up at the ceiling. "Will she always be a slave?"

"I hope not. Sometimes God has plans for us that override the plans of men."

Kneeling down in the dusky light, Mother reached for the special wooden box she had brought with her, the box which at home she always kept locked and on a shelf I could not reach.

"What do you keep inside there?" I asked. The box had always made me curious.

"I have told you. Papers." She took a key from her waist pouch and put it into the lock.

"Papers about me?" I asked, drawing closer.

"Some of them."

"May I read them?" I asked.

"When you are older," said Mother. "There are also papers in the box about my brother, Frederick. That's why we must go to America."

She opened the box and pulled something out. I crawled over to take a look. Instead of papers Mother took out a pair of small wooden clogs with vines and bright-colored flowers painted on them.

"What pretty little shoes!" I exclaimed. "Were those once mine?"

"No."

"Then why do you keep them?" I asked.

"My mother wore them when she was a girl," she explained, holding the shoes out to me. "They are also a part of the reason for our voyage."

I put my hands inside the clogs and clicked them together.

"There are many things I have not shared with you, Monday. Where we are going, slavery is widespread. It has touched my own family. My own mother was enslaved."

A shiver ran through me. My mother had always refused to tell me about her childhood. So this was the secret she had been keeping! "Was your father a slave as well? . . ."

Mother shook her head. "My father was a de Groot and a D'Angola. Both families are free."

"But your mother . . ."

"My mother was called Mando. She was born in Madagascar. When she was very young, she was stolen from her family and sold. She was brought to America on a ship."

"Just like baby Monday," I whispered.

My mother's usually calm face looked pained. I clenched my fists. My insides boiled with anger.

"Who did my grandmother serve?" I demanded.

"A rich Hollander family who lived in New York. The family presented Mando as a gift to their young daughter."

"What was the gift?" I asked, not quite understanding.

"Mando was the gift," she said. "Mando was given to the young Hollander girl as a servant. And on that day, the Hollander girl gave Mando a gift, too—these wooden shoes."

I caressed the insides of the shoes, where Mando's feet had worn them smooth. "I suppose they were trying to be nice," I muttered grudgingly.

"None of it was nice," Mother snapped. "Besides, those shoes hurt Mando's feet. They were much too small. But the Hollander girl made Mando wear them every day, because she wanted to see her slave wearing her present. The family even had a portrait painted of their daughter with Mando kneeling at her feet. In the portrait Mando was wearing the shoes."

I hung my head. "How sad Mando's story is, Mother."

Mother's eyes lit up. "But that isn't the end of Mando's story. After living for thirteen years in the Hollander house, Mando walked away. She walked away along a river, never to return."

"Didn't the Hollanders go after her?" I exclaimed.

"Of course," she replied with a nod. "But they could not catch her. Mando knew every curve of the river. She had studied it. She knew where to hide."

"What did she eat?" I asked.

Mother smiled. "Cake. The family was having a party the night that Mando left. She took a big sweet cake out of the kitchen and wrapped it in a piece of calico. Then she put the bundle on her head. She also had the wooden shoes with her."

"Was she wearing them?"

Mother shook her head. "She had walked out of those shoes long before then. She put them in the bundle, too."

"But why? The shoes were useless."

"Mando never told me why she brought the shoes out with her. Maybe because they were one of the few things that really belonged to her.

"She followed the river until it became another river, which wound up into the hills. That's where she met my father, Sebastian de Groot. He lived with his family on a farm called Shingle Kill. They got married and had my brother, Frederick, and me. Frederick and I were born free."

"So the story has a happy ending," I said, tapping the shoes on the floor. I looked up at Mother. Her face was sad.

"Not quite," she said softly. "Do you remember my brother, Frederick?"

I nodded eagerly. Uncle Frederick had come on a ship when I was quite little. He had worn a round blue cap.

"Frederick was in the British navy," Mother said, twisting her hands.

"Is he still in the navy?" I asked.

Her eyes turned to stone. "No. Something very bad has happened to him. French privateers captured his ship and liberated the cargo. They took the British seamen as prisoners to Martinique. The white seamen they threw into a dungeon, but Frederick they sold."

For the second time that night, a pang went through my heart. "Oh, poor Uncle Frederick! Why?"

"Because he is a black person," said Mother. "The Europeans do not make slaves out of too many people that look like they do. Since most of their slaves are black, they thought that Frederick might as well be a slave, too."

I had begun to breathe very hard. My mother touched me. Her hands were cold.

"Where is he now?" I whispered.

"A slave trader brought him from Martinique to New York, where he was sold a second time. Though he has tried to explain that he was a free person when he enlisted in the navy, his owner will not be persuaded to give him his freedom." She swooped the clogs up, tossed them into the box, and slammed it shut.

"I can't let them do this to my brother, Monday. My mother, Mando, walked out of those wooden shoes. I will not let them force my brother's feet back into them," she vowed fiercely.

"How will you free him?" I asked.

"I have the papers that say who he is," Mother explained. "First I will go to Frederick's owner, a man named Kortwright. Then if necessary, I will go to court. Frederick has already sent a written petition to the Attorney General of the colony, presenting his case. But according to the letter he sent to me in care of Captain Boyd, he has not yet received a response. My brother needs me, Monday. Otherwise I would never go back to America."

I drew my knees up to my chin. "I'm scared, Mother."

She knelt down and hugged me. "Don't be afraid. While I am trying to help Frederick, we'll stay with my cousins the D'Angolas. They are wonderful people! Their daughter Viola is only a few years older than you are."

"But America sounds like such an awful place. It's where Mando wore the shoes that were too small for her and where they will not believe Uncle Frederick is the person he says he is."

"There, there," Mother said gently. "I am sorry to have frightened you. America is actually a very beautiful place," she assured me. "From the farm where I was born, you can see trees that touch the sky. And all day you hear the music of the river. And there are many good people who live there. You'll get to meet some of your family."

"Is our cousin Viola tall?" I wondered out loud.

"I haven't seen Viola since she was a small girl. What does that matter?"

"I only asked because you are so tall."

"My tallness comes from the de Groot side of my family. Viola is a D'Angola."

"She will tower over me anyway," I said, slipping down onto my pallet. "Why am I so short?" I complained. "People call you 'Giant.'"

"Maybe you are a giant on the inside," said Mother.

Mother spread a blanket over me. Then she lay down beside me. I warmed my feet in the folds of her skirt. In a special place next to our water pouch was my nkisi, my own small wooden god I had brought from home. I reached out and felt it with my finger.

"Try to think of pleasant things," Mother whispered. "Think of home."

I closed my eyes and saw spreading palm trees and the blue sea near my village. I have a green parrot named Portugal. He is staying at our neighbor's house while we are gone. My lemur, Owl, is so clever he takes care of himself. Our neighbor is also caring for our cow, which is white and has a big hump. There are red and yellow flowers that grow on the path by the small house where Mother and I live. On our trees we grow mangos . . . I did my best to picture it all and then to see in my mind the face of my best friend, Kiden Lado, who has just come of age and had a big party.

Mother rolled over.

"I saw that portrait, Monday," she said in a voice half asleep. "Once I went to a fine Hollander house to deliver a baby. A painting hung in the foyer—a girl with yellow curls, her young black servant was kneeling at her feet. The servant girl was wearing wooden shoes." She grunted.

"The owners of the house didn't know that the black child in the portrait was my mother."

Very soon, Mother was snoring. But for a long time I lay awake. My thoughts drifted from the sweet memories of home to the events of the evening. I had helped to bring a baby into the world, only to discover that her life would not be her own! Then Mother had revealed to me, for the first time, the brave and difficult history of her own mother, Mando, and shared the horrible news of Uncle Frederick's capture.

Holding tight to my nkisi, I sat up in bed. On the other side of the curtain, one of the Kendricksons stirred. Outside, the ocean was roaring. And from somewhere on the ship, I could hear a faint cry.

"Please watch over little Monday," I whispered in my nkisi's ear. "And please take care of Uncle Frederick, until Mother can get there to help him."

With each passing hour, the *Peggy* was taking Mother and me closer to the unknown.

Petition...
His Majestys Attorney General
of the Colloney of New York in North America
The Humble Pittion of Nero Corney...

Your Pittioner had the Misfortune to be taken by his Britanic
Majestys Enemy the French and carried into the Island of
Martineco where your Honour's Pittioner was condemned as a
lawfull Capture and of Course sold at Ppublick Vandue to a
Merchant of that Place:....The purport of this your Honours
Pittioner is to beg that your honour will take this your
Pittioner case into consideration and hopes your honour May
see it sutiable to his Majestys Laws that your Honours
Pittioner....May have my freedom.

From the petition of Nero Corney, an enslaved African, requesting his
freedom, addressed to Attorney General Kemp, circa 1759.

Chapter Two

Shortly before dawn, we were awakened by the sounds of weapons firing, loud footsteps, and screams. I had scarcely opened my eyes when a man with a musket lurched through our curtain.

"Vámonos!" he shouted. Rising to her feet, my mother grabbed my hand and we followed the man through the curtain. Another man with a long saber at his side stood over Mr. and Mrs. Kendrickson. The older couple was kneeling on the floor with their heads bowed. Mrs. Kendrickson's nightcap was crooked, and long gray hair flowed out onto her shoulders. The man with the saber pushed a knee into Mr. Kendrickson's back. The old man scrambled up and hobbled forward with his wife following. Mother and I walked out behind them onto the deck.

Another vessel had pulled alongside the *Peggy*. Captain Boyd and some of his sailors stood lined up at the side of the deck, while the captain argued with yet another man waving a musket. Men with rags wrapped round their heads carted the ship's cargo up out of the hold. I recognized one of the men taking the cargo as the captain's own— that same Spanish sailor with the shell earring.

"Pirates," my mother whispered in my ear. "One of the captain's men has joined their ranks."

A loud explosion came from below. I gasped and clung to my mother. She pulled me into the shadows, where in a huddle with the Kendricksons we stood frozen beneath the mast, hoping not to be noticed. A man in a large hat charged up out of the hold, waving a musket and dragging the Hollander sailor, Ten Eyck, by the scruff of his neck. Ten Eyck was howling and clutching his leg. The pirate hurled him across the deck, while the others in his party passed up bolts of cloth and casks of rum hand over hand. The sharp smell of smoke choked the air. Quaking like a leaf, I tried to disappear into the folds of Mother's cloak. For the moment, we were being ignored, but at any instant one of the pirates might grab one of us and hurl us across the deck or shoot us with his musket! I began to whimper. Mother squeezed my hand tight.

"Sh!" she whispered. "Be quiet!"

The pirates continued to empty the hold. Barrel after barrel came up. I found myself wondering which one contained Captain Boyd's kettles. The captain himself stood in the middle of the fray, shaking his fist and arguing. His men still stood in a stiff line, guarded by a trio of the outlaws, who threatened them with drawn sabers and pistols.

Standing on the other side of me, Mrs. Kendrickson made a slight noise and wobbled. Her husband caught her arm and kept her from falling. Four African men in torn clothing were being marched up out of the hold, carrying a body.

"God be with us," whispered Mr. Kendrickson.

"The Angolan man with the fever has died," Mother said, bowing her head.

The pirate in the large hat prodded the four men to the side, then, poking them with his musket, he made them toss the body overboard. My mother drew in a sharp breath as the corpse hit the waves, and I began crying.

"Peace be with the soul of the departed," prayed Mr. Kendrickson.

Over the commotion, I heard a baby's cry and something squeezed inside my chest. The Sudanese women were being led in a line out of their cabin. Their heads held high, clutching their few belongings, they walked toward the ladder. In the very back was infant Monday's mother, holding her child to her breast! The baby was wearing that same piece of linen in which my own mother had wrapped her. I cried out!

"Be still!" Mother warned.

Her warning came too late. My cry had caused the man who had broken into our cabin to again take notice of us.

"Negras, vámonos!" he shouted, waving his musket at Mother and me.

"No!" Mother cried. She backed further into the shadows, dragging me with her. I clung to her waist for dear life.

"Have pity," Mr. Kendrickson pleaded.

The pirate knocked the old man out of the way. I could hear the heavy sound of his boots. Suddenly I felt a rough hand on the back of my neck. The pirate had grabbed me!

"Let go of her!" Mother screamed, grabbing me back. "This is my daughter!"

For a moment, I was tugged between the two of them. My head began to whirl. I opened my mouth to scream, but I could not make a sound, I was so frightened. The clawlike hand dropped me suddenly, and I slipped to the floor clinging to Mother.

Captain Boyd had pulled the pirate off. "Leave those women be!" he yelled. "They are passengers! Isn't it enough that you have ransacked the hold? These Negro women are not part of the cargo—they are free people. Have some decency!"

"Estas Negras tienen libertad!" the captain shouted.

"Vámonos!" the one with the shell in his ear called from the other side of the deck. The pirate who had grabbed me clumped off. I peeked from where I'd been hiding behind Mother's skirt. As quickly as they had come, the pirates were leaving. They disappeared into the night, taking the enslaved ones with them. Little Monday's mother was prodded over the side and down the ladder to a waiting skiff. A few moments later, I saw her again, holding the baby tight, scrambling up a web of rope to board the pirates' own vessel. Captain Boyd spit and stomped off. "There goes my profit," he muttered.

The pirate ship left us, cutting a path into the waves.

"Where are they going?" I whispered, glancing up at my mother's face. "Where will the pirates take Monday?"

"We have no way of knowing."

"Will the pirates still make her a slave?"

Mother's head dropped. "It is best not to think on it."

"I thank the good Lord that they did not kidnap thee and thy daughter," Mrs. Kendrickson murmured. Her hand landed on my shoulder.

"Yes, we must be grateful," Mother said. She gazed at Mr. Kendrickson's face. The old man was resting his fingertips on the side of his head.

"Were you hurt when you were knocked down?"

"Nothing to mention," Mr. Kendrickson replied.

Mother came closer and squinted. "You have swelling there,

where blood is collecting beneath the skin. I'll help you take care of that."

"How kind," sighed Mr. Kendrickson.

The four of us walked back toward our cabin. The deck was littered with debris—a bolt of calico lay unfurled across the deck, leaked on by a smashed cask of rum. The captain's men trailed through the darkness, trying to set things right. Near the stairway to the hold, moonlight fell on a dark pool of blood. "You are needed, Mistress de Groot!" Captain Boyd called out from the stern. "We have a man wounded."

"Ten Eyck," Mother muttered beneath her breath. "I had almost forgotten."

"Run along," said Mrs. Kendrickson. "We will see that Monday is settled in."

"Thank you," Mother said, hastening away.

As I watched her tall form dart down the shadowy deck, a wave of terror swelled up inside me. Blinking away tears, I bit my lip so that the Kendricksons would not see me crying. I loved my mother more than any person on earth, more than anyone could love any creature. To think that only a short while ago, we had nearly been separated! Remembering the pirate's clawlike hold on my neck, I began to quake all over again. I would rather die, I thought, than be taken away from my mother. As if they sensed my distress, the Kendricksons moved in closer and each took one of my hands, flanking me on either side until we entered the cabin.

"I will fetch some herbs for a poultice for Mr. Kendrickson's head," I said, quickly ducking beneath the curtain.

"May I be of help?" Mrs. Kendrickson called.

"I can find them," I answered. In the darkness, I felt inside my mother's sack and pulled out the pouch in which she had stored her herbs and tinctures. I recognized the bottle of lavender oil by the smell. I also grabbed some dried sage and a small bottle of honey.

I hurried back to the other side. Mr. Kendrickson was lighting a lantern.

"I've torn a piece of my petticoat to wrap the medicine," Mrs. Kendrickson said, holding up a soft white cloth.

"I don't see what the fuss is about," Mr. Kendrickson said. He wagged his head a bit too vigorously. "Ouch!" he said, touching the swelling. "I suppose I did get a knock."

I uncorked the bottle of lavender oil. "The cloth must be damp," I told Mrs. Kendrickson. She dipped the cloth into a pitcher on the side table and wrung it out.

"Will that do?" she asked, holding it out to me.

I nodded and laid the cloth on my lap, then carefully crushed the sage over it, poured on a few drops of oil, and folded the cloth into a neat rectangle.

"Here you are," I said, offering the poultice to Mr. Kendrickson.

"Ah," said the old man, raising the folded cloth to his head. "The smell is most soothing."

"You should lie down," I suggested. "Sometimes people fall for no reason after they've been knocked on the head."

His eyes twinkled. Though I was unaccustomed to Europeans, the couple did not seem like strangers.

"I will take thy advice," said Mr. Kendrickson. "But first my wife and I must say our prayers."

"When you lie down, you might take a bit of honey on your tongue," I advised, placing the bottle on the side table. "Mother says honey cures everything."

"Many thanks," said Mr. Kendrickson. "What a kind child."

"And a brave one," said Mrs. Kendrickson. "Join us in prayer?" she asked.

"No, thank you," I said, backing toward the curtain. I reasoned that the Kendricksons' god was British. I was sure that I would not know how to speak to him, even though Mother had told me that Quakers often prayed in silence. "I'll wait for my mother," I said, disappearing to my own side of the room.

"Can't we do anything for thee?" Mrs. Kendrickson asked.

"I'm fine," I replied. Taking my nkisi in my hand, I wedged myself into a corner. Though I knew that I should give thanks for my safety, I could not bring myself to say the words. Mother and I had not been harmed, but others had. Why should I thank my god, when he had let the pirates take little Monday? When he had let the sick Angolan man die in the hold? Could he not have found it in his power to protect us all? I had begged him to keep Monday safe, but he hadn't. Tears spilled over my hands and onto the wooden god's head.

When Mother returned to the cabin, I was still awake. The ship had begun to pitch more fiercely, making my stomach rise to my throat.

"Captain Boyd wants to see us in his cabin," she said, kneeling down next to me. Gently unprying my fingers from around the nkisi, she put the god next to her box and covered my shoulders with a blanket. "Come along. I've already roused the Kendricksons."

Summoned unexpectedly for a second time, our band of four trooped out onto the deck. The sun was a blinding half globe of light rising up out of the distant horizon. The sea buffeted us about as we made our way to the captain's cabin.

"Could Captain Boyd not have waited to have an audience with us?" grumbled Mrs. Kendrickson. The old woman grabbed onto Mother's arm to keep from falling, while her husband charged forward, pressing his hand to the side of his head.

"Have patience," Mr. Kendrickson said. "It must be important."

Mother knocked at the cabin door and Mariner Ten Eyck opened it. We scurried inside and the wind made a final whooshing sound before the door banged shut. In the center of the room, the captain was seated behind a mahogany desk, writing in a book. When I'd first met Captain Boyd, his hair had been dark, but one year it had turned all white. The quarters were quiet, the only noise coming from the scratching of his quill. Even the caged red lemur Captain Boyd had brought on board to be his pet was quiet.

"Well, well." Captain Boyd looked up and laid down his quill. "Quite an eventful night we had."

"Truly," said Mr. Kendrickson.

The captain peered at him. "Head feeling okay? Mistress de Groot told me that you suffered a knock."

"Fine as rain," said Mr. Kendrickson.

The captain stood up. He was a tall person, but not as tall as Mother.

"I thought I should apprise you of our situation. We are just off the Turks Islands and approximately ten days from our destination. Though the pirates raided the galley, they did leave us some salted mutton. Since the scoundrels did not manage to locate our water store, we will have enough water, which of course will still need to be severely rationed. In practical terms, as you would guess, this voyage is a complete loss. However, I deem it fortunate that they spared the lives of the crew, and I am also grateful for your safety."

His gaze rested on Ten Eyck and then on Mother.

"Thanks to Mistress de Groot's skill, our one casualty has been dealt with and Mariner Ten Eyck still has his leg."

The captain smiled and Ten Eyck grunted.

"It is unfortunate that one of the African men died," Mr. Kendrickson spoke up.

"Oh, one of them always dies," said Captain Boyd. "Good that the pirates liberated the rest under the circumstances. They're no use to me dead. And if they'd been left on board, they'd have starved to death."

"But you just said that there was food," volunteered Mrs. Kendrickson.

"Food for us," said Captain Boyd.

Mother's arm shifted on my shoulder. I glanced up at her. Her jaw was tight.

"Will that be the end of it then, Captain Boyd?" she asked tersely.

Captain Boyd stared at Mother for a long moment. "I see that you are miffed with me again, Mistress de Groot." He turned to the Kendricksons. "She insists that the slaves be treated as people."

"Well, they are," said Mr. Kendrickson. "Had my wife and I known that you deal in that trade, we would not have booked our passage on the *Peggy*."

"Heavens, man, don't be so moralistic," the captain scoffed. "I only dabble in the trade. I don't have people lined up toe to toe in the hold, do I? But if a couple of fine specimens are available at a good price, who am I to turn down the opportunity? Someone else will make the profit if I don't."

The Kendricksons were silent. Mother lowered her eyes. Captain Boyd bent down and smiled at me.

"I am very happy to see that you are not hurt, Monday," he said in a kind voice.

"Thank you for rescuing me from that pirate," I said.

"Not at all," the captain said, rubbing his whiskers. "I couldn't let those pirates kidnap my favorite eleven-year-old. After all, you and your mother were two of the first passengers ever to travel on the *Peggy*."

"Is that true?" Mrs. Kendrickson murmured, turning to Mother.

Mother nodded. "My mother's family was born on Madagascar. I had always wanted to visit."

Captain Boyd chuckled. "Mistress de Groot and I met in New York. She talked me into hiring her as a nurse for the sailors. Then three months later when we were to set sail, she showed up with an infant and a nanny goat. It turned out I needed her," he said with a twinkle in his eye. "We weren't out to sea for five days before I was flat on my back and Mistress de Groot had to leech me."

I flinched. Though I knew it was a healing thing, I hated leeching.

"The girl has inherited her mother's skill," Mr. Kendrickson volunteered. "She made me a poultice that has taken the aching from my head."

The captain gave me an approving nod. Then he crossed to his desk and took out a silver flask. "Shall we share a bit of brandy, to toast the end of this night?" he asked, raising the flask.

"None for us," said Mr. Kendrickson.

"You?" he asked, peering at Mother.

She stared straight ahead. "No."

The captain took a swig. Ten Eyck grunted and crept forward. Mrs. Kendrickson let out a huge sigh. "May we go now?"

The captain bowed swiftly. "Yes, of course. Just wanted to see that everyone was in one piece and to tell you about the mutton."

Mother made a sharp turn toward the door. The captain was there to open it. He reached into his pocket and pulled out a banana. My mouth watered.

"This is for you," he said, handing the fruit to me. "I've been hoarding it for my lemur. But you shall have it instead."

"Thank you," I said, bowing swiftly.

He smiled at me with his lips, but his gray eyes were like a stormy sea. "Run along," he murmured.

Outside, the wind was calming down. "I have a fruit!" I said, skipping along the deck. I turned back to Mother. The Kendricksons looked weary.

"Do you think you might offer a piece of fruit to anyone else?" said Mother.

"Would you like some?" I asked the old couple.

"No, my dear," Mr. Kendrickson replied.

In the cabin, I gobbled down my fruit, then collapsed beneath my blanket. Sleep burned behind my eyes.

In the days that followed, I stared into the indigo sea, looking for pirate ships and thinking of the Angolan men and Sudanese women who had been captured that night. My dreams were filled with the cries of babies and the thud of something falling into the water. Every morning, I asked my nkisi to take care of little Monday.

Mr. Kendrickson and I fished. Once we caught a sea trout. Mother also kept me busy studying Arabic. I practiced writing the characters in the margins of her old grammar book, *The English and Low-Dutch School-Master*.

From the deck, we watched schools of porpoises play. When the sea was calm, jellyfish floated on the surface. Then one day the sea changed from an indigo color to a light green, which Captain Boyd said meant that the water was shallower. On a warm afternoon, when we were fishing, Mother and I and the Kendricksons noticed a golden glow on the horizon.

"Is that land we see?" Mother asked.

"We are out too far to see land," said Mr. Kendrickson. "That is only the glowing of the land."

"I remember it from our previous voyage," Mrs. Kendrickson told us.

As the brilliant glow beckoned, I thought of how happy I would be to stand on solid earth and decided the first thing I would ask for would be a mango.

One morning, I woke up to the chiming of bells and the sounds of horses' hooves. My mother was already awake and dressed and was stuffing our blankets into her bag.

"Hurry," my mother said, handing me the drab skirt.

"I would rather wear something less dull, when meeting my uncle and cousins," I complained. I thought of the favorite dress I'd packed from home. The cloth was from India and a deep yellow color.

"You will wear this," she said, pulling the skirt over my head. "And remember, do not speak out of turn." Her eyebrows came together in a worried frown. "I will talk for both of us."

"Is there some rule against children speaking in public in these colonies?" I asked, hastening to button my blouse. "Certainly I may greet my uncle and cousins?"

"Of course," Mother said, handing over the bonnet she'd bought for the trip.

She deposited our large leather bag in a spot just outside the door and then came back for me and for the wooden box. She gave me her sack to carry. The Kendricksons had already vacated their half of the cabin.

When I went outside, I discovered that our ship, which for so many weeks had been a lonely speck in the blue sea, was now in a crowded, bustling harbor. What a variety of sights there were! There were spreading green trees, and lots of red brick houses, towering spires, and a building capped with a dome. And the sounds! Hundreds of mariners' voices, the calling of gulls, the hooves of the horses trotting on shore, and the same melodious chiming that woke me up. My mother pulled me forward. Now grouped up with the Kendricksons, we followed the captain across the plank and walked ashore. Though the sun was quite bright, the coolness of the air made me shiver. My eyes darted. There were almost as many faces on shore as there were ships crowded into the harbor. Since New York was British, I had expected most of the people to be quite pale, but there were many who had our color. I caught the eye of an old man with white hair, pulling a cart.

"Is that my cousin?" I asked.

My mother shook her head. We were still trailing behind the captain. "Cousin D'Angola is not so old as that," she said. "Nor does he sell wine. Besides, he will not have heard of our ship's arrival. His instructions for us were to go to a tavern known as the Sign of Two Cocks Fighting, where the owner will get word to him that we have arrived."

Having followed Captain Boyd, we found ourselves in the midst of a cluster of tables. Behind the tables official-looking men greeted people with luggage. I reasoned that the ones with luggage were passengers just like we were.

Captain Boyd directed us to a table under a tree, where a stooped-looking man was seated. Unlike the officials at the other tables, this one was wearing no wig.

"These are the Kendricksons," Captain Boyd said, steering the old couple in front of us.

The man peered up. His naked head had very little hair but an unfortunate number of scabs.

"Where have you come from?" he asked.

"England," said Mr. Kendrickson. "We are bound for Lebanon Springs, New York."

"How long will you be here?" the official demanded.

"We hope to settle," said Mrs. Kendrickson. "This is our second voyage."

He gave the Kendricksons a sour smile and waved them on.

Mrs. Kendrickson turned around and pressed my hand. "Goodbye, my dear. Godspeed."

"If thee and thy daughter are ever in the vicinity of Lebanon Springs, please visit us," Mr. Kendrickson said to Mother.

Mother bowed. "Thank you. We have enjoyed your company."

The official cleared his throat loudly. "Next, please—"

"This is Mistress Leslie de Groot and her daughter, Monday," Captain Boyd announced, nudging Mother to get her attention.

The scab-headed man looked us over from head to foot. "And where did you pick them up?" he asked, turning to Captain Boyd.

"We are citizens of Madagascar," Mother spoke up.

She reached into her pouch and produced some papers. The man squinted his eyes at them.

"From Madagascar, eh?"

"Yes," said Mother.

He frowned. "You're free people, both of you?"

"Yes."

He clucked his tongue. "Paid for your passage?"

"Yes."

He lifted his eyebrow. "My, my . . ."

He peered again at the paper.

"Very difficult to read," he remarked. "I've found that the penmanship of officials in Madagascar and other such places does little credit to the King's English. I hear it's an island of outlaws."

"It's only that some pirates like to come there," I blurted out.

He leaned into my face. His breath was foul. "Over here, young women can be thrown into the stocks for talking too much." I backed away in fright and Mother put an arm around me. "Teach her to keep quiet," he said, shaking a finger in Mother's face.

"Yes, of course," Mother said quietly.

"Let's see what you've got with you," he said, pointing to our leather bag.

My mother hoisted the bag up onto the desk. He opened it and stuck in his nose.

"Something smells."

"Curry," she said. "I brought it as a present for relatives."

"And this lump of indigo—is it a present, too?" he asked, rummaging inside.

"Yes."

He lifted a scraggly eyebrow. "That must have been dear."

"I bartered for it," my mother said, with a trace of impatience.

"Not smuggling any rum, are you?" he persisted.

My mother raised herself to her full height. "Certainly not."

"And what's this?" he asked, grabbing my mother's sack from me.

"My mother's medicine sack," I spoke up.

"Look here, my man," Captain Boyd interrupted. "I commissioned Mistress de Groot to help us on the *Peggy*. She is a midwife knowledgeable in all sorts of medical matters. She works for me regularly in Ft. Dauphin."

The official's eyes popped. "So this woman acted as a surgeon?"

"One of my men was shot in the leg. She kept the wound free of infection," said Captain Boyd.

"May we go?" Mother asked, taking her bag back.

"Not just yet," the official said. He pointed to the wooden box. "What's in there?"

"Only some family documents." She looked at the captain. "If you could prevail upon this gentleman—"

"Yes, let's get on with it!" Captain Boyd barked. "This woman is related to the D'Angolas. They're residents of the city."

"And known to me," the official grumbled, poking the box toward my mother. "What will your business be here, may I ask?"

"We are on a visit."

"And when will you be returning to Madagascar?"

"I am not certain," Mother replied. "As soon as possible."

"Put your marks down on the list," he said, shoving forward a quill and paper. My mother wrote her name. Then she handed me the quill. The official rapped his fingers with impatience, but I took my time, signing with my fanciest signature. Snatching the paper up, he waved us on.

My mother and I picked up our luggage and followed Captain Boyd to a place on the side.

"I wish you good luck in helping your brother," said the captain. "The *Peggy* will be going out again sometime in the next month. I'll post a notice. If you can't get hold of a newspaper, look for a sign in the window of Judah Hays's shop in Hanover Square. They usually know where I am at the Sign of Two Cocks Fighting, if you need to get a message to me."

"Two Cocks Fighting . . . that's where I'm to leave word for my cousin," Mother murmured.

"If you wait for a bit, I can escort you there," Captain Boyd offered. "You might have trouble finding the right place. Every other door is a tavern."

"No, thank you," Mother said. "We're eager to be on our way." Mother walked on without looking back. She had hoisted the big bag up onto her shoulder and tucked the box underneath one of her arms. I carried the sack on my head, bumping along behind as we made our way through the crowd. On a strip of green across the way, red-coated soldiers played a game of knocking down carved figures with a ball.

"That official certainly kept us long enough," Mother remarked. "More than likely, he was looking for a bribe."

"What's wrong with his scalp?" I asked.

"Nothing that a few papaya skins wouldn't cure," she replied.

Suddenly we were nearly run over by a pale skinny youth in a much too large three-cornered cap and high black boots. Perhaps the boots were also too large, for as he was charging straight toward us, he stumbled, butting his head into my mother's lap! His three-cornered cap fell off, revealing a head of hair of a strange and foreign color—a deep, dark red such as I had only seen in flowers, never on a person. As quickly as he had stumbled, the youth stood and made a bow to us.

"Please excuse me," he said, stuffing his hat back on.

My mother smiled and so did I. There was something about the boy that was comical. "Can you direct us to the Sign of Two Cocks Fighting?" Mother took the opportunity to ask.

"You must be looking for Dr. D'Angola!" he replied.

"Why, yes," my mother said in surprise.

"He told me to look for a towering woman with a girl," the youth explained. "I am Werner Dietrich, the doctor's apprentice. Dr. D'Angola is at the tavern. In the market we heard about the *Peggy*'s arrival."

My mother breathed a sigh of relief. "Thank you so much," she said. The boy reached for the large bag on Mother's shoulder, but Mother did not give it over. She also insisted on carrying the box. I, on the other hand, was only too glad to let him carry the heavy medicine sack. As we walked down the road after the youth, I observed how, with his free hand, he took pains to tuck every one of his bright hairs beneath his cap until not one was visible.

"If I had such feathers, I would show them off," I whispered to my mother.

The boy stopped by a wagon drawn by a black horse. There was a seat up front for the driver and benches along either side in back. Mother and I climbed in the back, while he settled our bags for us and then took the driver's seat. I looked up and down the street as the horse got off to a trot. Right away we approached one of the buildings with a spire that I'd seen from the deck of the ship.

"Is that a palace?" I asked, craning my neck up.

"God's palace," my mother answered.

"Which god lives there?" I asked in awe.

"The Christian one, whose name is Jesus," she replied. "It is a church."

At home Mother and I went to a church also, but it was only one small room. Mother had been brought up to believe in Jesus. She taught me to believe in him, too, but also let me keep my household god.

"Trinity Church!" the boy called out, turning round from his perch. "And over there is the British fort."

"He has the accent of a German," my mother remarked. "When I was growing up here, I knew several German families."

"What is the difference between a German and a British?" I asked.

"They are from two different places," she explained, "though their countries are in the same part of the world."

"How does our cousin come to have a German boy in his house-hold?" I wondered aloud.

"How do any of us come to be where we are?" replied Mother. She tucked her wooden box beneath her skirts.

To Be SOLD *by Ebenezer Grant in* HANOVER-SQUARE

Best Geneva, Madeira and other wines; old Jaimaica rum and Brandy by the five gallons... Spices of all sorts, black pepper, rhuburb pounded, Best Durham Mustard, Loaf sugar, currants and Raisins; best Scotch snuff in bladders; anchovies and capers. Candles by the box.
TWO LIKELY NEGRO WENCHES, about 18 years old of Age, one with a child about a year and a half old to be sold.

From the *New York Mercury,* April 16, 1759.

Chapter Three

The tavern was a short distance away, situated between brick houses, with a good view of the beach. Here the road was lined with crushed seashells. Beneath a sign featuring two roosters, a man in a blue waistcoat stood waving his hat.

"Cousins!" he cried out.

When the wagon came to a stop, he rushed behind and grasped my mother's hand. "Leslie! What luck! And this must be Monday! Thank you, good Werner!" he added, shouting up at the boy.

My mother and I climbed out. Though she towered above her cousin, he made up for it in girth—his powerful-looking arms and legs were the size of tree trunks. And his mouth was a marvel. For when he smiled I saw that where three teeth should have been were three pieces of gold!

"Monday"—my mother poked me—"say hello to your cousin Paul D'Angola."

I made a low bow. On his shoes Cousin D'Angola wore large silver buckles.

"I am so pleased to have you with us," Cousin D'Angola said, helping Werner take out our luggage. "How was your journey?"

"Spanish pirates boarded the vessel when we were in the Caribbean, taking all but a little food."

"Then I am doubly thankful that the two of you are safe," Cousin D'Angola said, pressing my mother's hand into his own.

"The captain went out of his way to place us under his protection," Mother said grimly, "yet he sees the loss of the Africans in his cargo only in terms of his profit. When I met him years ago, he had not been corrupted."

Cousin D'Angola clucked his tongue. "Few among them have the strength to turn away from that loathsome trade."

"What are you talking about?" I asked, tugging on my mother's elbow.

She straightened my bonnet. "Not to worry."

"Certainly not," said Cousin D'Angola, pulling two striped sticks out of the pocket of his waistcoat. He gave one of the sticks to me and the other to Werner, who right away started to lick it.

"What is it?" I asked.

"Peppermint," Mother said. "It's sweet, like sugar cane."

I licked the peppermint stick as Werner had done. The taste was sweet, but also peppery. "Very good," I said.

"And the third one is for Viola," Cousin D'Angola added, patting his pocket. With a few words out of earshot to Werner, our cousin motioned Mother and me toward the tavern. "The owner is a friend of mine. He's saved a table for us. We'll wait here while Werner goes on his errand."

We edged our way in through a crowd at the door. Men of all descriptions were lined up on either side of a pit, in which two white cocks had been set to claw at each other. The men shouted and cheered. I turned away.

"Just an ordinary cockfight," Cousin D'Angola said, waving us to a table in the back. "You should see it on New Year's Day! They line them up for hours. The whole tavern is just one big merry slaughterhouse."

I made a face and he laughed.

"Don't tell me you're squeamish?" he teased. "Can't be squeamish in America."

Refusing to see the humor in his remarks, I sat down at the table next to Mother.

"Would you like something to eat?" Cousin D'Angola asked, leaning across the table.

My stomach growled with hunger.

"How about some chicken stew?" he suggested.

I shook my head. That was the one thing I didn't want!

"May I have a mango?" I asked politely.

"No mangoes in New York," he replied. Reaching into his pocket he tugged at something. I was hoping for the other peppermint stick, but instead he presented me with a small, white, shriveled thing.

"Have this bit of apple. It's from my own tree. My wife, Pearl, slices the fruit, then strings it up to dry."

I wrinkled my nose. The fruit my cousin had given me looked like paper.

"It would be polite to try it," said Mother.

I took a bite. It was quite tart.

"Please, may I have some water?" I asked, trying to hide my distaste.

"Never drink the water in town," Cousin D'Angola instructed. "It's brackish."

Just as I was about to give up on having anything, our cousin ordered cider and skinny meat things called sausages, which I gobbled up so quickly that I burnt my fingers and tongue. Though I was sure she was hungry also, Mother ate nothing.

"I have spoken with Frederick," Cousin D'Angola volunteered, downing his cider. "Lately Kortwright has him in service at his lumberyard, which is right here in town. I've sent Werner round to ask after him."

Mother took a small sip of cider. "Thank you, cousin. How does my brother seem?"

"Determined. Frederick has faced war, don't forget."

"But this is a different kind of battle," Mother murmured.

"Never fear, Leslie," Cousin D'Angola said, reaching for Mother's hand across the table. "You'll find a way out for him."

"I pray that I can," she said. "I have his papers. My intention is to entreat Kortwright in person."

"If anyone can manage to help Frederick, you are that person," said Cousin D'Angola.

At that moment, a roar went up near the entrance and a man wearing a gnarled brown wig hurried past with a bleeding rooster. Just behind him, with his hat jostled crooked, was Werner.

"Frederick de Groot is at the meal market," Werner announced breathlessly. "If we hurry, we might catch him."

"Is it far?" Mother asked, getting up quickly. "I haven't quite yet gotten my bearings."

"Two streets over," said Cousin D'Angola. "Better to go by foot than to be blocked by carts and wagons. The market is busy this time of day."

I had to run to keep up with those two. Werner was to follow at his own pace with the wagon. The street was lined with shopwindows stuffed with things I wanted to see, but I could not stop to look. We passed two women and a boy standing on a block. A white man stood before them, shouting out a price: "One hundred pounds for the lot! A bargain . . ." I stopped to stare at the horrible scene. One of the women caught my eye—she looked frightened. Mother dragged me onward. At last Cousin D'Angola stopped at a corner.

"This is the place," he said, catching his breath.

Mother's frantic eyes searched the crowd and rested on a thin, dark man balancing three thick planks of wood across his back. In order to balance the planks, he was bent over, bearing the heavy-looking wood toward a wagon.

"There he is," she whispered.

Rushing out into the street, Mother was almost run over by a high, grand-looking thing drawn by white horses. Her skirt got splattered, but she seemed not to notice. The thin man had found a way of resting by touching the side of the wagon with his head. A helper on top lifted the wood onto a pile plank by plank. The man's arms dropped and he slowly stood up as Mother approached him.

"Frederick . . ."

He stared at her blankly. Beads of sweat covered his face, and on his neck there was an ugly scar that looked like a brand. Mother came closer.

"Don't you know me?"

The man shook his head, as if waking from a dream, and then he caught sight of Cousin D'Angola. His face suddenly alert, he smiled.

"Oh, Leslie! You've come all this way!"

"Of course," said Mother. She held her arms out and the two of them hugged. Uncle Frederick almost seemed to collapse.

"Forgive me," he said, straightening himself up. "It's very warm today."

"The least they can do is provide you with fresh water," Cousin D'Angola muttered angrily.

"We have water in the wagon," said Frederick. He glanced up at his helper and then at the lumberyard. "I can't take but a moment. This delivery is expected." His eyes then fell on me. They were set in so deep you could hardly see them.

"Hello, Uncle Frederick," I said, offering my hand.

"You are Monday, aren't you? I hardly recognized you."

"I would not have known you," I confessed.

"But you remember me?"

"I remember your blue cap. The one that you are not wearing."

Uncle Frederick smiled sadly. "We will talk again. You'll tell me all about elephants."

"Oh, I don't have an elephant," I said. "But I can tell you about lemurs."

My uncle turned to Mother. "A fine child. You're taking a risk by coming back."

"There was no other way," said Mother. "I will do everything I can for you. Kortwright must have a conscience."

"Do not endanger yourself," he entreated.

"He can't hurt me," Mother said.

"She's tough, all right," chimed in Cousin D'Angola.

Uncle Frederick cleared his throat and hugged my mother again. His companion from the wagon was now waiting beside him. "I must get on with work." Before turning back toward the lumberyard, his eyes rested on me. "Do take care . . ."

Across the way, Werner was waiting with the wagon. Mother and Cousin D'Angola moved away swiftly.

"Is someone going to hurt us?" I asked. "They won't make us slaves, will they? Because Uncle Frederick is?"

Mother turned to me sharply. "Certainly not. Let me hear no more talk like that."

She held my hand tightly as we crossed to the wagon and Cousin D'Angola held her arm.

"It's frightening how thin he is," Mother said in a half voice. "He's suffering."

"There, there," Cousin D'Angola comforted her. "Seeing you, his spirits must be lifted."

We climbed into the wagon and my mother and I took seats on one of the benches. As the opposite one was filled with our bags, Cousin D'Angola crowded in next to me. Caught between him and Mother I felt squashed.

"What was the strange-looking high wagon that passed?" I asked. "The one with the door and white horses."

"That was a carriage," said Cousin D'Angola. "Only the very rich have them. Once there was a Hollander who was so large that he and his wife could not fit in the same carriage on Sunday."

"I think I've heard this tale," my mother said. "How did this lord and his lady manage?"

"Why they had two carriages, of course," Cousin D'Angola said, smiling at me with his gold teeth. "One for him, which was completely taken up by his bulk. And another for her."

"Was the lady also large?" I asked.

"Very tiny," he replied. "In fact, alone in her own carriage, she was lost."

I laughed. Mother gazed out at the busy street.

"So you are called doctor now, cousin?" she murmured politely.

"Some are pleased to do so," he replied.

"I recall your fascination with healing plants."

"It's paid off," said Cousin D'Angola. "They've actually had me over to consult at the hospital. Thanks to a remedy I devised using the seed capsules of the Virginian anemone, I have gained a reputation for curing toothaches."

Turning his way, Mother touched her own jaw. "A misery I've often suffered."

"You and all the world, Leslie," he said.

"Not me," I offered from my squashed position. I smiled to show my teeth. "My mouth is perfect."

"And I am sure that your heart is perfect, too," said Cousin D'Angola.

The wagon was going at a good speed. Leaving the river-front behind, we wound our way across the city and came to a swamp.

"How old is Viola?" I asked.

"Fifteen," said Cousin D'Angola, "almost a woman. You'll meet her in just a few minutes. Our house is across this cripplebush."

I leaned forward. Tall swamp grasses lined the narrow road.

"What is this road called?" I asked.

"Some call it the Negro Causeway," said Cousin D'Angola. "But we call it 'the way to go out.'"

"Why is that?" I asked. "Where are you going out from?"

"Oh, out from the city, I suppose," he mused. "Out away from the fancy houses, out of the swamp . . ."

"And where does 'the way to go out' lead?" I persisted.

"To my house. And to the homes of our neighbors. Most of the people who live around here are Africans like we are."

"Do slaves live here, too?" I asked.

Cousin D'Angola shook his head. "No one here would ever keep slaves. We are free people, though many of our friends and the people we are connected to are in bondage."

The road narrowed to a small opening, overgrown with swamp trees. Werner urged the horse on and we were hurled through the heavy growth and into a brilliant green clearing.

"I remember this," Mother said softly.

We passed rows and rows of plantings leading to a yellow house with a tiled roof, a wide door, and small glass windows. The yard outside it was plucked clean, except for two spreading trees with white blossoms and a bed of tall red flowers.

"How beautiful!" I exclaimed.

Mother smiled for the first time since we'd seen Uncle Frederick. "Indeed—and how our cousins' tulips have increased!"

As the wagon came to a stop, the top half of the door to the house swung open and two women appeared, waving. As we were getting out of the wagon, the younger of the two women opened the bottom half of the door and ran out. I knew that she had to be Viola. Sturdily built like her father, but not at all towering, Viola had wide-set golden eyes and cheeks with great dimples. Her mother, whose eyes were the same unusual color, walked toward us.

"I am your cousin Pearl." The woman of the house greeted us with open arms. Her head was wrapped in a lovely piece of dark green cotton with a red stripe running through it. Her skirt was the same color.

"I am Viola," her daughter said, snatching the peppermint stick Cousin D'Angola had taken out of his waistcoat. Her round face spread into a smile. "If you don't mind my saying so," she volunteered, "you don't look at all like Africans. You're dressed just like the British."

Mother let out a great whooping laugh which seemed to go on forever as Cousin Pearl and Cousin D'Angola joined in. They continued to laugh as we walked into the house, though I thought my cousin's joke was very rude. It wasn't my fault that Mother had forced me to wear the drab skirt! Looking pleased with herself, Viola strolled in sucking her peppermint stick, while Werner stayed to take out our luggage.

Every surface of the room was adorned with colorful fabric—the backs of the chairs, the table, and even the walls. In a spot by the window was a loom.

"You have become an artist, Pearl," my mother said, admiring the hangings.

"Everyone wants to be buried in one of her shrouds," Cousin D'Angola boasted.

Cousin Pearl smoothed her green skirt. "The dead have no choice in the matter," she said, lifting an eyebrow. "It is their families who are pleased to send them off to the next world in something colorful. And I am pleased to assist them."

"I didn't mean to be irreverent," Cousin D'Angola said. "I do my best to keep them from dying by pulling rotten teeth."

"Pay no attention," Viola whispered in my ear. "They're not really arguing."

The D'Angolas settled us right in. I was to share a bed with Viola and my mother would sleep on a bed next to the fireplace in Cousin

D'Angola's small office. Viola took me next door to the kitchen, to get me a fresh drink of water drawn from the well. Cousin Pearl was shucking the largest oysters I'd ever seen. And on the hearth a sort of punch was brewing.

"It's the week of Pinkster," Cousin Pearl explained. I sniffed the brew while Viola dipped me some water.

"What is Pinkster?" I asked.

"A festival celebrating Pentecost. In the Christian calendar, that is the time when the Holy Spirit comes down from heaven to earth. It happens seven weeks after Easter. It's the best time of year here. All the flowers are coming out." Cousin Pearl wiped her hands and crossed the room to stir the punch.

"The punch is for the party we're having tonight. But the oysters we'll eat for dinner."

I followed Viola outdoors to see the rest of the place. There were two other buildings, one for storing fruits and the other for the animals.

"How many goats do you have?" I asked, peering into the animal house.

"We have no goats," said Viola.

"Too bad," I muttered.

"We do have two cows." She beckoned me inside. One animal was only a calf and the other was a great white thing.

"Is this the mother?" I asked, putting my arms around the white cow's neck.

Viola nodded. "Her name is Swan."

I kissed the cow in the spot between her eyes. "She reminds me of my cow," I said, "only my cow has a big hump on her back."

Viola cocked her head. From beneath her white cap, a hundred small braids peeked out. "Do you have wild cats in Madagascar?" she asked.

"In the jungle," I replied, "but I have never seen one. We do have long wicked lizards called alligators. An alligator killed our calf."

"Do you have suitors in Madagascar?" she prodded.

"I am not of age yet," I said. "Do *you* have suitors?"

"Yes," she said, her face dimpling. "But nobody knows about it except Werner. Today Werner took him a message. Father and Mother don't know it, but tonight he is coming here."

"What is your suitor's name?"

"Sampson."

"Is he very strong?" I asked eagerly.

"He is a powerful person in every way," Viola declared. "I would die for him."

"I can't wait until I have such feelings," I said, with my heart fluttering. "What is Sampson's other name?"

Viola lowered her eyes. "He does not care to have another name. Someday we will be married and he will take mine."

"He must love you very much," I said, trying to envision the strong young man. "I suppose he gives you many presents."

"When he can," Viola replied.

"At home my friend's suitor gave her family a goat," I told her. "Maybe Sampson will make you the gift of a goat," I suggested excitedly.

"Please hush," she said, grasping my wrist. Her eyes looked pained. She took her hand away from my arm and I rubbed it.

"I only thought a goat would make a good present, since you don't have one," I muttered.

Viola let out a soft sigh. "Please promise me that you won't tell anyone about Sampson and me."

"All right," I agreed, rubbing once more the spot where she had grabbed. There had been a forcefulness in her touch that was almost frightening.

"I probably shouldn't have told you about us," she murmured, "but I long to talk to someone. Werner is the only one who knows."

"Why not your parents?" I asked.

Viola shook her head. "They would never approve."

"GRANT to *Marycke* a free negress, widow of Lawrence, a negro Dec 12, 1643 conveys a certain piece of land to the west of Swagersland, stretching next to *Antony Portugees* land...in all amounting to 6 acres. *Richard Nicolls* Gov."

"*Richard Nicolls*, Governour to *Christoffell Santome.* Oct. 15, 1667 confirms a grant to *Christoffell Santome*, a free Negro made to him by *Director Stuyvesant* in 1659-60..."

Chapter Four

Dinner was oysters, a corn porridge called sappan, and boiled greens gathered from the field. While we were at the table, I noticed that on the mantel the D'Angolas had their own wooden nkisi, much larger than my own, with pieces of metal driven into the stomach.

"The metal hammered into the god's stomach releases the power of his anger," Cousin D'Angola explained. "I drove in three new nails when I heard about Frederick de Groot's situation."

Mother sighed and laid down her fork. "To think that my brother has been so deprived. His capture by the French I can accept—after all, he was in the military—but that Kortwright would keep him in bondage knowing full well . . ."

"Did Kortwright know Frederick before?" Cousin Pearl asked.

Mother nodded. "Our family home at Shingle Kill borders some of Kortwright's country holdings. My own father used to provide his overseer with barrels. If Kortwright does not know Frederick personally, he certainly knows of our family."

"The indignity some of our people suffer is so vile I can hardly fit it into my mind," Cousin Pearl said.

"There's lots of indignities, all right," Werner said, reaching across Mother to grab another oyster.

"It would be polite to ask Mistress de Groot to pass the platter," Cousin Pearl said, shooting him a look. "And please do take your hat off at the table."

Werner popped up and took off his hat. But as soon as he sat down, he reached across Mother again and swooped up another oyster.

Cousin Pearl sighed. "It is a tedious task to teach the young."

Viola and I glanced at each other and burst into giggles.

"But one that is necessary," Mother said, jabbing me with her elbow.

"I think we are boring them," Cousin D'Angola said with a good-natured smile. "What would you like to talk about?" he asked, turning to Viola.

"Presents," Viola said mischievously.

Mother chuckled. "Of course. Please bring out the gifts, Monday," she directed me.

I ran to the study and pulled the gifts out of the bag—indigo for Cousin Pearl, the curry for Cousin D'Angola, and for Viola a bracelet made of shells.

"Oh, how useful!" Cousin Pearl exclaimed. "I've always wanted to weave a sky-blue shroud."

"Why not think of the living?" said Cousin D'Angola. "I should like a new waistcoat that color. I fancy an indigo blue rather than the pale blue waistcoat I've got."

"I believe this is my gift," said Cousin Pearl. "Therefore, I'll decide what to do with it."

"Very well," Cousin D'Angola said, taking a whiff of his curry. "I'll use this to spice my own dish."

"And I will let everyone enjoy the beauty of my new bracelet," Viola said, rolling her eyes.

Mother and I exchanged a glance of amusement. Then I noticed Werner. He was sitting politely with his hands in his lap.

"I'm sorry we didn't bring you anything," I said to him.

"No bother," said Werner. "I'm not part of the family."

"You certainly are!" Cousin D'Angola protested.

"We've adopted you," said Cousin Pearl.

"I'll share my curry with you," Cousin D'Angola said, reaching across to pat Werner's hand.

"And I will make you an indigo shirt," Cousin Pearl promised.

Werner's face turned as red as his hair. "Thank you so much," he said. "But I really don't need it."

Viola laughed. I gulped down the last of my corn porridge. I very much liked my American family.

For the party that evening, the table was moved to one side. Cousin Pearl's punch was served in a bowl and there was also a keg of ale. A man arrived with a leather drum and began to sing and beat out rhythms. Though I did not know any of the songs, the rhythms sounded familiar.

Then came the guests. Each time someone arrived, Viola whispered something to me about them.

"See that soldier?" she gossiped. "He's an Irishman. Once he came here with his jaw swollen three times its size. He howled when Father yanked out his tooth. Werner put a poultice of hot gruel and hot fat on his jaw to fight back the swelling. The soldier howled again. Just imagine!

"See that couple holding hands? They get to see each other only once a month. They live in different places, because they're bound to different masters.

"Oh, that blind woman there is named Bett . . ." And so forth.

My eyes darted around the room, taking everyone in. How strange that a soldier should howl at his tooth being yanked, I thought. How sad that the couple lives apart. The way the woman rests her head on his shoulder, they seem to belong together—I wonder if they have children. The blind woman is touching Mother's face, as if they might know each other—how surprising!

Then Viola pointed out the neighbors who had come: a man named Anthony Portuguese, his wife, Maria, and three grown sons; then another person named Simon Congo. Viola explained that both families had farms bordering the acres that the D'Angolas owned.

The grownups talked and drank and ate and laughed. At one point Werner offered us a sip of ale out of his cup. Viola and I took a taste and both agreed it was awful.

"Why do you hide your red feathers?" I teased Werner. He was wearing his hat in the house.

His cheeks turned almost the color of his hair. "Because someone might notice me."

Suddenly all eyes turned to the door. An agile-looking young man in a speckled vest and blue serge trousers was making an entrance. Stuck beneath one of his arms was a thin bundle of papers.

"Sampson!" Cousin D'Angola called out. He hurried to the door. "I hadn't hoped to see you this day."

"My master De Peyster is dining out," the young man said. His voice was so deep and clear that it carried across the room. "I am on my way home from market."

Cousin D'Angola chuckled. "The market is quite out of the way from here, I'm afraid. And so is the place where you live."

The young man's eyes twinkled. For just an instant, he glanced at

Viola. "Imagine, I've come and gone to the market so many times, but I seem to have forgotten how to get back."

"You're a clever one," Cousin D'Angola said. "I hope you can spend some time with us."

"I can stay only for a short while, but I could not miss your party at Pinkster." He bowed in the direction of Cousin Pearl. "Hello, Mrs. D'Angola," he said, extending the slim bundle he had with him. "I have a newspaper."

"A newspaper!" exclaimed Cousin D'Angola, snatching the bundle. "Listen up, everyone! Sampson has brought a copy of the *Mercury Gazette!*"

Everyone crowded around. Even the drummer stopped drumming.

Viola stood stiff as a board. Her hands were shaking. So this was her suitor, I thought. There was certainly something quite striking about him. Though lithe in stature, Sampson had strong-looking arms and shoulders and a round face with a high forehead. His nose was broad and his mouth generous. His eyes, which were unusually black, sparkled with humor and intelligence.

"Why don't you go over to him?" I urged, nudging Viola. "He is the one, isn't he?"

"Quiet!" she said sharply.

Cousin D'Angola had opened the newspaper. Several people looked over his shoulder.

"Read it to all of us!" shouted Anthony Portuguese.

"Where shall I read from?" asked Cousin D'Angola. "The front or the back?"

"Perhaps from the back," Sampson said. "There's news there that might interest us."

"Well, here—" Cousin D'Angola said, shoving the paper his way. "You read it."

"What is it?" I pestered Viola. "Why are they so interested?"

"The writing in a newspaper tells us about what's going on in the city," Viola explained, "as well as other places. It also lists goods that the merchants have for sale."

"Like kettles?" I asked.

"And other things," Viola replied. "It isn't very often that we get to have a newspaper in the house. Not that many of them are printed and they're grabbed up by the rich people."

Sampson had begun to read. Everyone was quiet.

"Run away from Judah Hays, of the city of New York, Merchant, on Tuesday the 23rd, a German servant woman named Dorothy Sisivey . . ."

"I know a Sisivey!" Werner piped up.

". . . had on when she went away a striped linen josey and a blue half-thick petticoat. She is remarkable by having lost one part of her right thumb. . . ."

"I don't understand," I whispered to Viola. "What is it about?"

"A servant woman has walked away from her indenture," Viola said.

Sampson continued reading: "Run away from Staten Island, a Negro man named Tom, speaks good English. Run away at the same time a Negro boy, named Harry, 14 years old, speaks good French and has lost one of his fore teeth. . . ."

"Why have all those boys run away?" I whispered to Viola.

"They are slaves, of course," she whispered back.

"There's seeds of resistance in walking away," Simon Congo commented. "Say what you like, we're all in chains as long as one of us is."

Sampson stopped reading and bowed his head. The rest of the room grew silent.

"Put the paper away, Sampson," Cousin D'Angola said, bustling to his side. "Have some of Pearl's good punch. Let those that know how to read take a look at it for themselves."

As Sampson made his way to the table, Viola took a few steps in his direction. I got up and began to walk toward him too. There was something about the young man I was drawn to, not so much his rich-sounding voice but his face, which reminded me of someone, though I couldn't quite figure out who.

"I'll introduce you to him," Viola said, reaching back for me. But out of nowhere Mother had appeared and placed a firm hand on my shoulder.

"Come with me, Monday. You must rest from your journey."

"It's still very early," I protested.

"Do as I say. A child deprived of sleep can become ill."

Feeling cheated, I crept upstairs to Viola's room and lay down in my shift on my cousin's mattress. There was no way I could make myself sleep with a party going on right below me. It wasn't fair that I should have to stay upstairs all alone. Fortunately a few moments later, Viola appeared. She sat down beside me and a loud rustling came from the bed.

"Your bed is very noisy," I commented.

"It's stuffed with corn husks," she mumbled, staring up at the ceiling. "Sampson has left. He could not stay long."

"I wish I could have met him," I said.

"When he and I are married, Sampson will be your cousin," Viola said with a dreamy look in her eyes.

"I think your suitor is very handsome," I said. "And he must be rich, since he has a newspaper."

Viola smiled sadly. "The newspaper didn't belong to Sampson. It belonged to his master."

"His master?"

"Sampson is a butler at the home of a wealthy shipper." Tears spilled out of her eyes. "He does not own himself."

"Your suitor is a slave?" I exclaimed.

She nodded.

"But he wears such fine clothes," I protested, scarcely able to believe what my cousin had told me.

"What does that matter?" she said. "They only dress him that way to match the furniture. He cannot choose his own wardrobe. He cannot choose anything about his own person." She tore off her kerchief and threw it down on the bed.

"When I was four years old, bugs rained out of the sky," she muttered.

"What kind of bugs?"

"Locusts. Everyone hated them but me. Mother says they will come back in a few years. By the time they do, I will be married to Sampson."

"How do you know that?"

"It's a feeling I have deep inside," said Viola. "I just know it." That instant a big black bug skittered across the room. Quick as lightning, Viola jumped up and stamped it unconscious.

"Poor bug," I said. "Is it one of the locusts already?"

Viola picked the bug up with a glass. "Only a kackerlach. New York is full of them. Mother uses their wings to make glue."

She put the glass on the windowsill and then began to pick her braids with a comb. There was an oval mirror on the door of the clothes cupboard.

"I have always loved him," she confided.

"Why doesn't he run away?" I asked. "So many people in the newspaper did."

"And many of them will be caught," said Viola. "Do you know what they do to people who try to steal themselves?"

Her golden eyes narrowed. "They strip off their clothes for all the world to see. Then they tie them to a cart drawn by an ass. At every corner in the city, they stop the cart and give the person nine lashes. Do you understand what that is?" she said bitterly. "A person cannot even walk after such a beating. From such punishment a person can die."

"How awful," I whispered, cringing at the gruesome description. "My mother's mother ran away, too. But she was never caught."

"That would be hard for Sampson," said Viola. "So many people in the city know who he is. They have seen him wait table or buy things at the market for the De Peysters. He cannot simply leave. His face would be recognized. It's as if he is kept on an invisible leash."

Remembering the intelligent face of the striking young man, I was filled with sadness. "Sampson reminds me of someone," I said. "I think I have seen him somewhere."

"That's impossible," said Viola. "You live in Madagascar. Were you born there?" she asked.

"Oh, no," I replied. "I came with Mother on a ship. It was the *Peggy*."

"And who was your father?" she inquired.

I shrugged. "Mother knows, but she won't tell me. Only that he is dead."

"Everyone has a right to know who their father is," said Viola.

"I've asked and asked Mother," I told her. "But for some reason she doesn't want to speak of it."

"There is some mystery about your birth," Viola said, snuffing the candle out. "I heard my mother and father talking about it when we received news that you were coming to visit."

"What mystery?" I asked, sitting up.

"My parents had not seen your mother for some time," Viola said, snuggling down onto the mattress. "Then they heard from a neighbor who works on the ships that their cousin Leslie de Groot had gone to Madagascar and that she had a child with her."

"That's precisely what happened," I said. "Why is that a mystery?"

"Because they hadn't heard about your birth, or for that matter they don't know who your father is. Don't you think that's strange?"

"How do you know all this?" I asked, bristling.

"I overheard my parents talking," Viola said. "I often spy on them."

"I see," I said coldly. "Well, for your information, my mother is not strange. Some people are very private about their lives." I turned away from her.

"I'm sorry to have annoyed you," Viola said gently. "I'm sure there's some explanation. There's probably some part of the story that my parents know that I haven't heard."

"You shouldn't spy on other people's conversations," I said, parroting what Mother had taught. "If you repeat what you've heard them say, then it is gossiping."

"Gossip can be hurtful," Viola muttered, stretching her toes. "Sampson has been hurt by it a great deal, because people gossip about his mother."

"What do they say about her?" I asked.

"I can't tell you," Viola said, with a wicked gleam in her eye. "That would be gossiping."

I giggled. "You can whisper in my ear," I said.

Viola drew closer. "She killed her baby," she said softly.

I pulled away quickly, horrified by what I'd heard. "That's not funny."

"I didn't mean it as a joke," Viola said, her voice turning serious. "The story is tragic. Sampson's mother is named Dina. She is also in bondage. Both Sampson and her husband had been sold away. There was one child left, a baby girl. Rather than bring her up in slavery, Dina jumped overboard when she and the baby were on a boat going to New York to their new master."

My heart began beating faster. "Is that how the baby died?"

"Yes," Viola said softly. "She was drowned when Sampson's mother was trying to escape. The baby's name was Easter."

I blinked away tears. "How very sad for Sampson to lose his sister. Did he ever see his mother again?"

"That's the lucky thing," Viola said. "Dina was first bought by the Hoglants, but later the De Peysters needed a cook. They knew Dina from when she and her husband and Sampson lived with the Philipses. So the De Peysters bought her, and since they were the ones who had bought Sampson earlier, Sampson and his mother got to live together after all."

Sinking into the mattress, I turned my face to the wall. Viola had rattled off so many names, I could no longer follow the story. But I did know that it was sad. Since leaving Madagascar it seemed as if almost all joy had drained from the world. I thought of the meeting with my mother's brother.

"Uncle Frederick looked very thin today," I whispered. "And on our ship there was a baby who was taken by pirates."

"You are overtired," Viola said, stroking my arm. "You must rest."

But my cousin tossed and turned all night, causing the noisy mattress, along with my troubled thoughts, to keep me awake.

The next day was Sunday. After a meal of fried apples and bread,

Mother, the D'Angolas, Werner, and I fit ourselves into the wagon. We were going to a service at Trinity Church. Cousin D'Angola was driving. Cousin Pearl had with her a large bunch of tulips from the garden.

"Do you not still attend the Dutch Reform Church?" Mother asked.

Cousin Pearl nodded. "Indeed. But my husband has some tricky reason for taking us to Trinity."

"We'll be there in two shakes of a lamb's tail," Cousin D'Angola called out as the wagon jerked forward.

When we arrived at the grand-looking church, bells were ringing out from the high tower and lots of people were walking in. Outside the church was a large grassy yard filled with cut stones. Viola told me that the English buried their dead there.

"Our dead are buried not far from here at our very own grave-yard," said Viola.

Once inside, we took seats in the back with other people of color. Werner sat with us. I also noticed a girl my own age in our section who had light brown skin and yellow hair. Viola whispered to me that some part of the girl's parentage was English as well as African.

I found the singing in the church quite unexciting—it was slow and the people had little expression on their faces. But I could not hear enough of an instrument called the organ. One moment its sounds were as sweet as a bird's and the next they were as frightening as thunder. At one point during the service, Cousin D'Angola leaned over me and Viola and tugged at my mother. "There's Kortwright at the communion rail!" he whispered, pointing to a pale, slight man in a powdered wig. "I thought we might find him here." My mother clenched her fists.

"Be patient, Leslie," whispered Cousin D'Angola. "After church we'll intercept him."

When church was over, Cousin D'Angola and Mother looked in vain for Mr. Kortwright. "Perhaps he left by another entrance," Cousin Pearl suggested.

"Do you know where he lives?" asked Mother.

"Everyone knows that," replied Cousin D'Angola.

"Then let us meet him at his house," said Mother emphatically.

"Do what you must," said Cousin Pearl. "I will wait with the children at the graveyard."

"Stay in that one spot," Cousin D'Angola cautioned. "Pickpockets and ruffians do not respect the Sabbath."

"Are there thieves in New York?" I asked.

"Oh, it's full of hooligans," Werner informed me. "Just last week some gentry were beaten over the head outside of the college."

"Hush," said Cousin Pearl. "You'll frighten her."

Mother climbed up to the driver's seat next to Cousin D'Angola. I stared after her. "Mr. Kortwright won't hurt Mother, will he?" I asked Cousin Pearl.

"She could squash him like a bug," Viola volunteered.

"Let us spend some peaceful moments while we are waiting," Cousin Pearl said, avoiding my question.

Viola, Werner, and I followed Cousin Pearl up the street and entered a small courtyard carpeted with grass. Set into the ground in neat rows were gleaming cobblestones collected from the banks of the river. Some had markings scratched on them. Others were circled by seashells. Cousin Pearl walked toward one in the back and laid down her tulips. "These stones mark the graves of our dead," she murmured.

"My grandmother is buried here," Viola explained. "She died a year ago. My mother still mourns her."

Viola, Werner, and I walked among the other graves. I stopped at a large gray stone and knelt down to touch it. The stone gave off warmth. In front of the gravestone, someone had left a pink conch shell.

"How odd that you should choose this place to stop," Viola said. "It is where Sampson's father is buried." She knelt down and touched the stone too.

"How did he die?" I asked timidly. I had already heard of one tragedy in Sampson's family. I hoped not to hear of another one.

"Smallpox," Viola replied. "There was an epidemic shortly after Sampson's family was separated."

"Can you see the dead?" Werner asked, stepping up behind us. "I can."

"I certainly cannot," I said. "Nor would I want to. I would be afraid to see a dead person."

Werner shrugged. "If I close my eyes tight, I can see my mother and father, the way they looked before they lost their scalps."

"Their scalps?" I exclaimed.

"Indians," said Werner.

"India is in our part of the world," I said. "How did Indians come to these colonies?"

Viola plucked a weed growing next to the stone. "He's not talking about that kind of Indians. He's talking about Iroquois. His parents were killed in a raid. Father found him wandering around in the meal market."

"The Indians can't find us here, can they?" I asked, glancing around nervously.

Viola shrugged. "The ones in the city are friendly," she said. "Werner's family lived up the river."

"Then how did you get here?" I asked the boy.

"Had to get work somewhere, didn't I?" he said. "So I came to the city and the doctor took me on."

Cousin Pearl was back by then. We wandered out onto the street.

"Why is Mother taking so long?" I asked.

"Perhaps Mr. Kortwright has invited them to come inside," Werner said with a snort.

"If he has, I'm sure it is the first time Mr. Kortwright has done such a thing," Cousin Pearl muttered.

At last the wagon came bumping down the street. Cousin D'Angola waved us to get in.

Mother was now sitting in the back. Her face was expressionless.

"Well, what happened? Is Uncle Frederick free?"

"Kortwright refused to listen to me," she said in a steely voice. "He slammed the door in our faces, then forbade his servants to answer."

"What will you do?" Cousin Pearl asked.

"I will not give up," said Mother. "Tomorrow, I'll go to Kingston. The de Groots were well known there. It might be that I can find someone in a position of power who might intercede for Frederick."

She turned to me. "You'll stay here with our cousins."

"Without you?"

"Don't worry," Cousin Pearl said, touching my hand. "We'll have a good time together."

An ache welled up in my throat. I missed Mother already.

In the Store House in New Street Viz.

Empty Casks
a Large Parcell of Rubbish
80 Pine Boards
14 Oake D°.
a small Parcell of boards
a parcell of John Hoops &c.
A Large parcell of old & som new Staves
a parcell of old Rope
6 boxes of Pipes
a parcell of Files
3 Large Iron Salt Panns

On the manner of Philipsburgh 12th February 1749
Negros Viz:

Ceasar, Dimond, Sampson, Prijor, Flip, Tom — Men

Atha, Abigal, Maßy, Dina, Sue — Women

Venture, James, Charles, Billy — men not fit for worke

Tom ab.t 9 years old
Charles 9 d°
Sam 8 d°
Dimond 7 d°
Hendrick 5 d°
Ceasor 2 d°
Harry 9 months — Boys

Betty 9 yrs old. A Girl

Cattle Viz:
6 Worken Oxen
12 Milch Cows
9 3 & 4 y.rs old heffers, steers & bulls
9 2 ..... Ditto
6 - 1 ..... Ditto
30 Sheep Home Lambs
19 hogg. & 8 piggs
Horses Viz:
3 Stable Horses
o horses in the Woods
18 Mares & young horses

2 Silver Tankards
1 D°. mugg
6 New Silver Spoons
6 old Ditto
1 Silver tea pott
6 Silver forks
1 D° pepper box

(In the Garrett) April 19th 1750
6 flax Spining wheels
2 Woll D°
1 old Gun
Some Wool & Tow
a Miners pick &c
4 Siths & 2 handles
a flax Reel
a p° of old Scales & weights
Some old baskets & old Cask
a tin Cullender
2 small old brass kettle
a D° Skillet & old chafin dish & a small mortar
1 old tin Lanthorn
2 small Earthen potts
some Further
a Large Iron horse
2 old ox chains
1 Leap Nett
a parcell of Hops
a parcell of old Ditto
2 small flitches Bacon

Chapter Five

The following morning, we took Mother to the harbor, where she was to take a packet boat upriver to Kingston.

"I will be thinking of you every moment, daughter," she said. "Be obedient."

"Yes, Mother," I promised. She was clutching the waist pouch into which she had put Uncle Frederick's important papers. "I hope that you are able to help my uncle."

She kissed me lightly on the forehead, then stepped onto the boat. Suddenly, I felt as if I might cry. Instead, I swallowed hard and I waved at her from shore. Long after the boat was on its way upriver, I stared at the water.

"Watch this trick," Werner said, taking three plums out of the picnic basket Cousin Pearl had brought with us. He tossed the plums high above his head and caught them over and over, until the three pieces of fruit made a spinning arc in the air. "Very good, Werner!" Cousin D'Angola shouted, clapping.

Werner winked and tossed a plum my way. I caught it and laughed.

"Now she's in a better mood," said Cousin Pearl.

"And a good thing, too," said Viola. "It's still Pinkster. Are we going to Philipsburg this year?" she asked, turning to her father.

Cousin D'Angola smiled broadly. "We're going today. Your mother and I planned it as a surprise. I'd like to pay my respects to old Charles. And I hear that the king of Albany is visiting!"

"Who is the king of Albany?" I asked.

"The best drummer in the whole world," Viola exclaimed. "When you hear him, you can't stop dancing."

"Here's a boat going that way," Cousin D'Angola said, directing us down the dock. "Monday's visit with us wouldn't be complete without the Pinkster celebration at Philipsburg."

"Does my mother know about this place?" I asked.

"I'm sure she must remember it," said Cousin Pearl.

"I recollect that Leslie was called there as a midwife from time to time," added Cousin D'Angola.

"What sort of place is it?" I asked curiously.

"A vast place," said Werner, stretching his arms out.

"A family named Philipse owns it," explained Cousin D'Angola. "But they're renting it out, since the old lord died."

"There's a manor house on the property," said Viola. "Of course we can't go inside there. Most of the people we know live in the little cottages on the place."

"Tenant farmers," Cousin Pearl interjected.

"Not all," Viola said, giving me a sidelong glance. "Some of the people who live there are slaves. They run the mill and make ship biscuits. Sampson told me all about it. His father used to be the boatman who took the ship biscuits to the warehouse in New York."

Cousin D'Angola peered at her curiously. "It sounds like you had a lengthy conversation with young Sampson."

"We spoke at the Pinkster party," Viola said, avoiding his gaze.

We stopped in front of a packet boat. We waited until a group of British sailors boarded.

"I hope that Philipsburg will not be a sad place," I said. The talk of slavery there made me nervous.

Cousin D'Angola waved his hand. "Not at Pinkster. Everyone is merry then."

A roar of laughter came from the bow of the boat. The sailors were passing a bottle.

"Perhaps they're bound for Philipsburg as well," Cousin D'Angola said, leaning in confidentially.

"They've started celebrating already," Cousin Pearl said, wrinkling her nose.

I squinted at their canvas clothes and round blue caps. "My uncle Frederick wore a cap like that."

"A lot of good it did him," grumbled Cousin D'Angola. "It's taken Leslie working her fingers to the bone for that slaver Boyd to make this voyage to rescue her brother. Not to mention the cost of her expenses while she's here. We don't see any British naval officers speaking up for Frederick, do we? When the day comes for choosing sides," he declared, "I will step over and call myself an American."

"Hush!" scolded Cousin Pearl, cutting her eyes in the sailors' direction. "It is dangerous to talk such treason."

For about an hour, our small ship sailed on up the Hudson. Sun shone on the water, making it look silver. Cousin Pearl had packed the remains of some bread she'd flavored with small red fruit called whortleberries. She divided the bread among us. But before I could eat my piece, a strong breeze tore it out of my hands and some gulls coasting alongside us swooped down upon the water to fight for it. As we turned into an inlet close to the coast, I heard high, thin sounds in the distance and saw another church.

"Guess who is buried beneath the floor there," Cousin D'Angola called, pointing to the church.

"Who?" I asked.

"The lord who took up a whole carriage," he answered.

I nodded, for I remembered the story. "Does he also take up the whole church, now that he is buried?" I joked.

"Ha, ha! Not even he had that much bulk!" countered Cousin D'Angola.

As we navigated further up the inlet, the high, thin sounds grew louder. "Are those the bells from the church that I hear?" I asked.

"Those are pipes," said Viola. "At Pinkster there are all kinds of music."

The closer we came to the shore, the louder the music became, for drums had been added. Viola and I began to tap our feet. And when one of the crew leapt off onto the wharf, to secure our landing, I felt the urge to jump off too. The scene that met our eyes was so merry! The place was thick with people leaping and running in circles and waving long, flowering branches in the air. They had wrapped their heads with pieces of bright-colored cloth, and the ground where they danced shimmered pink with fallen petals.

Cousin D'Angola and Werner climbed onto the dock and helped Cousin Pearl, Viola, and me out of the boat. The group of

British sailors got out as well and headed straight for an ale stand. Our party climbed a small slope toward more level ground where a band of revelers danced in a crooked line, carrying a rope made of flowers. The dancers ran toward us, encircling me and Viola. One of them, a pale-faced man wearing a red cap with bells on, nearly fell into me. For a moment I was frightened. But when I saw Viola laughing, I knew that it was a game.

"Run!" she cried, breaking through the flowered rope.

I ducked under and ran after her. The merrymakers chased us toward a bridge, trying to capture us. I tripped, and a small girl with many coils of braids snatched off my bonnet, placing a wreath of flowers on my head instead.

"Come on!" Viola said, pulling me up. "Let's dance!"

We entered a throng of people prancing around a tree that was wrapped in fluttering cloths. The music—a drum, a fiddle, and some high-sounding pipes—kept getting faster and faster. I could have kept going forever, but Viola made us drop out.

"A blister on my toe has gotten the better of me," she said, yanking her shoe off.

"Rest for a bit then," Cousin D'Angola said. He sat down and patted her foot. "Look—here comes the king!" he exclaimed.

A large man in a plumed hat marched forward and took his place behind a long drum. The throng rushed to surround him. "Is he really a king?" I asked.

"We make him king for the day," Cousin D'Angola said, laughing. "He really is the best drummer in the colonies."

When the king began to play, the other musicians put down their instruments. At first he played softly. But then his music grew louder and louder. The drum sang and talked when he played. Then a woman began singing in a deep voice.

Death's chill is gone,
The spirit abides,
Be merry all!
'Tis Pinkster.
Dance with the drum,
Sing with the pipe,
Be merry all!
'Tis Pinkster.

"I like the drummer best," said Cousin Pearl.

"I like the singer," said Viola.

When the music stopped the crowd cheered. The man with bells on his hat shouted out: "Huzzah! Huzzah! Long live the African king from Albany and long live the singer!"

Having both taken off our shoes, Viola and I stood up.

"I am thirsty," she announced.

Cousin D'Angola gave her a coin. "Buy cider and cakes for you and your cousin over there by the mill. Then meet us at the cottage where Charles stays. Your mother and I will be there."

Viola bought us cider and cakes from a stand in the shade of a long open building. She took me inside and showed me a huge configuration of spindles, wheels, and flat stones that, when harnessed to the power of the river, turned grain into flour.

We then went again to watch the revelers dancing around the tree. The dance had seemed jumbled when Viola and I were a part of it. But watching from the outside, it had a wonderful order. Legs of people—young and old, black and white, some with strong boots and some shoeless, their ankles belled or beribboned or covered with white stockings—all treading a path in the earth, stepping in time but never on each other's feet.

"There is some entertainment over there," Viola said, pointing to a clearing on the other side of the bridge. Two men tossing swords back and forth to each other had claimed it as their spot and a crowd was gathering. I saw Werner sitting almost beneath them. Rushing over to see for ourselves, Viola and I passed a woman roasting a lamb on a spit.

"Do you think that she has some goat?" I wondered, my mouth watering.

"Who wants meat when we already have cake?" said Viola, dragging me forward.

"Please sit, gentle people!" a loud voice sang out. A man with one earring and a patched vest waved his arms in the air.

"As soon as our jugglers are finished, there will be a play."

"Oh, good!—a play!" exclaimed Viola. She nudged her way up front and found spaces on the ground next to Werner. "I have seen three plays here—I wonder which one they'll put on."

"What is a play?" I asked. "I have never seen one."

"A show where people pretend," Viola said, stuffing the last of the cake into her mouth. "Whatever happens, just remember it isn't real."

The sword jugglers had finished their performance. Werner cheered with the crowd.

"Hear ye, hear ye!" the man with the earring shouted. "This be the plays of Philipsburg!"

"Huzzah! Huzzah!" the crowd roared.

"I hope it's not the play about all the Dutch lords," Viola grumbled. "That one put me to sleep. And the play about the tomb of Christ made me cry."

"Hear ye! Hear ye!" the master of ceremonies sang out. "This be the play of Cuffee!"

Viola clapped her hands. "This is my favorite! The play of Cuffee is truly frightening!"

A girl Viola's age ran out to the front of the crowd. Her costume was a dress of red tatters. "I am the fire!" she cried, stretching her arms to the sky. Making wild motions, she ran in a circle.

"Are you the good kind of fire that warms my feet in the winter?" shouted the man with the bells on. "Or are you the evil kind that rages below?"

The girl moved her arms again wildly. "I am the evil kind of fire," she announced.

Suddenly a man with a fiddle leapt to the front.

"And who be you?" demanded the one in the bell cap.

"I be Cuffee!" said the man. Then he began to play on his fiddle one of the sweetest songs I've ever heard.

I leaned toward Viola. "Is Cuffee a king from Albany also?" I asked, thinking the fiddler was as good as the drummer.

"No, Cuffee was owned by one of the lords Philipse. The lord brought Cuffee from Madagascar to be a slave," Viola whispered. "He worked here at Philipsburg and also in the lord's warehouse in the city. Some people say that slavery made Cuffee so angry that he tried to burn down the whole of New York!"

"The whole thing?" I gasped.

"All of it," Viola said firmly. "Father didn't believe that Cuffee did it. But the judge did."

"I've heard the story, too," Werner joined in. "The British caught him and burned him alive at the stake."

The actress portraying the fire began to dance, while the actor who was Cuffee kept playing the fiddle. Then suddenly two men jumped out from behind a tree and wrestled Cuffee to the ground. While one of them took his instrument, the other tied his hands. The actress ran out into the audience, waving red ribbons in her hands.

"Would you like to be part of the fire?" she asked Viola and me, thrusting ribbons into our faces.

"Yes!" Viola said, grabbing a ribbon for herself. "We'll be in the play." My cousin pulled me up off the ground. I was trembling with excitement, but I also felt somewhat frightened. Seated on the ground watching us were hundreds of strangers.

"When they lead Cuffee forward, we will dance around him with our ribbons," the lead actress whispered to us. "We will dance closer and closer to him until he dies."

"He won't really die, will he?" I asked nervously.

"Of course not," Viola said, jabbing me.

"The fire never killed Cuffee anyway," the actress explained breathlessly. "Today his spirit is among us, descending to the earth like fire!"

The man portraying Cuffee was led forward. Though Viola had told me that the play was pretending, I felt very frightened.

"Guilty!" the man with bells on his cap sang out from the audience. "Burn him!"

Taking my cue from the actress and Viola, I waved the red ribbon in my hand and danced around. A drummer began to play loudly. We danced closer and closer to Cuffee, and the poor man began to curl up and scream. Then he fell into a heap.

The crowd let out a groan. Viola and I and the actress who played fire danced around the body. Just when I thought the play would be done, Cuffee sprang up again and took up his fiddle.

The crowd cheered and laughed. Cuffee played faster and faster in spite of the fire around him. Viola and I danced and danced until we were breathless. Then the actress who had enlisted us finally waved us away.

"Go sit down!" she said with a smile. "The play is over. Thank you!"

The crowd clapped and the man who had portrayed Cuffee took a bow.

"Come!" said Viola, grabbing my hand. "My parents will be waiting."

We put on our shoes. Then, leaving Werner behind, we found Cousin D'Angola and Pearl in a small house where they were visiting an ancient man called Charles. In the darkened quarters, Cousin D'Angola was rubbing one of the elderly man's legs with some liniment.

"Please say hello to our friend," Cousin Pearl instructed as we moved forward.

"Good day, Uncle Charles. I am happy to see you once more and in better health," said Viola, still breathing hard from our dancing.

"Thank you, sweet girl," said the old man. He squinted at me. "And who is this you've brought?—don't tell me—it's young Dina!"

"You are mistaken, uncle," Cousin D'Angola said. "This is someone you've not met before. Our young cousin named Monday."

I peeked back around. The old man's face was lined like a map. And when he opened his mouth to speak, I could see that he was practically toothless. Nevertheless, he spoke quite clearly.

"I know that pretty face," he said. "That is Dina."

"Who is Dina?" I asked.

"It's a common name," said Cousin Pearl.

"Sampson's mother has that name," Viola remarked. "Years ago she lived here at Philipsburg."

"Perhaps that's who Charles is thinking of," said Cousin D'Angola. He gently patted the old man's hand. "You are dreaming of the past, Charles."

Charles rubbed his eyes. "Of course, of course," he apologized. "Forgive me, young lady. When we get older, our minds wander."

"Don't give it a second thought," said Cousin Pearl. "Monday doesn't mind."

"I certainly don't," I assured him.

Charles's eyes shut and he began snoring.

"Time for us to go," Cousin Pearl said, tiptoeing out.

That night when we got back to New York it was raining. Long after Viola was asleep, I lay awake thinking of Mother. I hoped that her trip to Kingston was successful and that she would come back safe. Creeping into Cousin D'Angola's study, I found one of Mother's wraps and put it over my shoulders. Then I noticed that Mother had left the wooden box! Not only that; lying on top of her leather bag was the key she usually kept at her waist. Taking the box and key, I sat in front of the hearth.

A Choice Cargo of EUROPEAN and INDIA GOODS.

Juſt imported from *London* in the Ship *Dover*, and to be ſold cheap by ROBERT and RICHARD RAY, near the *Old Dutch Church*.

A Choice Aſſortment of EUROPEAN GOODS.

To be ſold at Publick Vendue, at Ten o'Clock on Thurſday Morning, the 19th Inſtant, at the Houſe of the late *Adolph Philipſe*, Eſq; deceaſed, on the Manour of *Philipſburgh*;

Four Negro Men, viz. *a Miller, a Boat-Man,* and *two Farmers; three Negro Women ; ſix Negro Boys, and two Girls ; Houſhold Goods, and all the Stock, conſiſting of* 40 *odd Head of Cattle,* 26 *Horſes, a Number of Sheep and Hogs, and all the Utenſils belonging to the ſaid Manour.*

Juſt imported, and to be ſold by FRANCIS LEWIS, in the *Fly, Alamodes, Luteſtrings, Ducapes, Damaſks, Mantua Silk, Grazetts, Paduſoys, Velvets, India Taffities, Grograms, Sewing Silks, Printed Calicoes, Muzlins, Cambricks, Long Lawns,* 7-8 *and yard wide Garlix, Check Linnens, Cotton Romalls, Bandanoes, ſtriped Ginghams, broad Shalloons, Tammies, Turkets, Starrets, Chivereets, and Ruſſels, Yorkſhire broad Cloths; and Kerſeys, ſtriped Blankets, Strouds, Coating, Penniſtons, Half Thicks, and Plains, Pipes, Florence Oyl, Italian Marble Tables and Mortars, Madeira Wine by the Pipe,* &c.

To be ſold cheap for ready Money or ſhort Credit, by MOSES CLEMENT, in the *Broad Way,* the following Goods ;

Fine embroidered Waſtcoats, embroidered Shoe Tops, Silk Mittins, white Gauze, Edgings, black and white Lace, white and coloured Thread, ſeveral Sorts of Fans, BoxCombs, Scented Powder, Mettal and Gilt Buttons, Silk Belts, Shammy Gloves, a large Aſſortment of Jewelry, and ſeveral other European Goods.

Photograph of an advertisement announcing an auction of Philipsburg Africans.

Chapter Six

Everything was quiet except for the ticking of a clock on the side table. I took the box into my lap. How often I'd wondered what was inside! Mother had told me about the papers regarding Uncle Frederick. She had taken those with her. And she'd shown me the wooden shoes once worn by Mando. But what else was inside the box? Viola's comment about my birth being a "mystery" had planted a nagging thought in my mind. What if there was something about myself that I did not know? I had long ago accepted knowing nothing about my father. But now that Viola had brought up the subject, Mother's secrecy in that regard did seem strange. If there was something about me inside the box, didn't I have the right to know about it? My fingers fumbled as I placed the key in the brass lock. It turned easily. I lifted the lid of the box.

There was much less inside than I had expected. The wooden shoes, a silver bell, and a book. The book was a copy of *The English and Low-Dutch School-Master*, just like the one Mother had handed down to me. Only this copy was more worn and the binding was splotched with water stains. I ran my fingers along the box's cloth lining in case I'd overlooked something, but could find nothing further. No mention of my father's name or anything else that would indicate that my birth was a "mystery." Resting my back against a chair, I absentmindedly opened

The English and Low-Dutch School-Master. Someone had used the empty margins in the book to write on, just as Mother had allowed me to do in her copy. Though the letters were splotched here and there, the penmanship was so exact I could still make it out. I knew for sure that it wasn't my mother's handwriting. . . .

Once on this river, I was having a child. The overseer had sent for a midwife. My husband and son waited outside the cottage door while the woman saw to me. She walked me around in a circle. I could not stop crying. 'Twas not the pain of childbirth that caused me to sob, but the pain of uncertainty. Three months ago our master had died and it seemed as if my family and all my friends were about to be sold. The master had lived in New York and his brother who had inherited did not need us.

All my life I had lived in the same place. I had known my husband from childhood. We were among the master's people who ran his estate. Some of us ran the mill, some of us farmed, some of us made ship biscuits in the kitchen and packed them in barrels to be shipped to the warehouse. My husband became the boatman. It felt almost as if we were free, since the master left us alone so much. But his death taught us that that feeling was a trick. Now I was giving birth and for the second time would bring into the world a life that would not own itself. That was why I cried so bitterly.

The midwife set me on my knees and rang a sweet bell in my ear. "That's so your child will come out wanting to hear your song," she said. I gazed into the midwife's eyes. She was my age and color, but she was free. I had known her once as a child.

A baby girl came out. The midwife was there to catch her before she fell to the floor. My heart burst with joy, but I was still crying.

"She is beautiful," the midwife declared. "I'll go fetch your husband and son. The overseer has given me sugar and chocolate for payment. If the child should develop colic, please send for me, as I have a remedy. But I hope that all will be well. Should I not see you again, God be with you always. In three months time I sail for Madagascar."

We loved our baby girl. Though her birth had missed it by a day, we named her for the Lord's most sacred Sunday.

For two months more we were a family. But then they sold my husband to Mr. Kortwright. I felt as if my arm had been torn off. They put a notice in the paper about the rest of us to be put up for auction. My clever young son was sold to Mr. De Peyster. My heart was torn out. After the auction there were few of us left, me and my baby and some of the old ones that nobody wanted. Then Mr. Hoglant came and said he'd take my baby and me, as his own wife had given birth and he needed a wet nurse.

The river shimmered with flowers the day Mr. Hoglant's overseer came to fetch us. There was no frolicking at Pinkster that spring. My baby girl was wrapped tight in a bundle. She was crying loudly. I asked the overseer if I might be excused to see the midwife, since she had a remedy for colic. He said that I might and waited at the dock for me. With my baby I ran to the cottage. When I returned the bundle was quiet.

I got on the boat bound for the city. I held the bundle tight. Whatever the world may think, I will always love Easter.

When I finished reading, I laid down the book and cried. What suffering there was in that writing! Clearly the notes had been made by a slave woman about the occurrences in her own life. Somehow, my mother had known her. I reasoned she must have been the midwife. Why else would Mother have kept the grammar book and its writings in her box all this time? But what was the name of the person who had written the tale, I wondered. Could she have been some relation of Mother's through her own enslaved mother, Mando? I leafed through the book for some further clue, but could find none. In the story, Hoglant and De Peyster and Kortwright had appeared as purchasers, but the names of the others had been left out. All except for one—Easter. I pondered on the name, trying to recall where I'd heard it before.

excellent oysters!

Pickled oysters:
open shells
wash clean
boil in pot
dry on dish
put mace, allspice, black pepper
and vinegar
boil again with
old liquid.
Skim off foam.
Put into a glass or earthen vessel—
well stopped to keep out air.
Oysters keep for years.

Traditional 18th-century recipe for pickling oysters.

Chapter Seven

"Hollow tooth to be stuffed!" Werner announced, rushing from the kitchen to the house waving a bottle of rum. I sat on a stool outside the barn, milking Swan, while Viola pitched fresh hay into the stalls. A woman wearing a black bonnet and moaning in pain from a swollen jaw had stopped to see Cousin D'Angola.

"Why does Werner need rum to stuff a tooth?" I asked Viola.

"Father says if you soak the stuffing in rum, it eases the patient's suffering."

I turned back to milking the cow. Since the D'Angolas had welcomed us in, I was doing my best to help out. But I was very worried. Mother had now been away for five days.

Cousin Pearl came out of the house, bearing on her head a basket of spun flax the color of pale sand. I had watched Viola and her mother make the dye for it using flowers called Queen Anne's lace.

"I will be working at the home of Maria Portuguese today,"

Cousin Pearl told Viola. "Please help me load the loom into the wagon. I will also need you to drive me there."

"Yes, Mother," said Viola. "Monday and I will help you directly."

I took the milk inside. Then, with Cousin Pearl's help, Viola and I brought the loom out and lifted it into the wagon.

"Change out of your work clothes," Cousin Pearl said, "so that you may say hello to our neighbors."

"Should Monday and I wait for you at the Portuguese home with the wagon?" Viola asked.

"No, you can drive back home again and begin the oyster pickling. Your father or Werner will fetch me before dark."

We hurriedly changed into clean skirts and aprons. Viola wrapped her head with a bright pink kerchief and put on the shell bracelet Mother and I had given her. Soon we were clattering along the road with Viola in the driver's seat and me next to her. Cousin Pearl sat in the back to steady the loom. Maria Portuguese's shingled house was quite close by. A plump woman with two long black braids, whom I recognized from the D'Angolas' Pinkster party, came out to greet us. When the loom was safely inside her house, Viola and I began the ride back home. Without the loom, the wagon was light and the horse went much faster. There was a strong breeze and I held tight to my skirt.

"What do you think is keeping my mother?" I asked.

Viola stared straight ahead. "What she is trying to do in rescuing her brother is almost impossible. She has to convince the officials that they must believe her over Mr. Kortwright."

"Mother is truthful," I argued.

"She is also a woman and an African," said Viola. "The better course would be for your uncle to run."

"I thought you said that it was too dangerous to run," I reminded her.

"I am changing my thinking on that," Viola said.

"I only hope that Mother is safe." I reached into my pocket and pulled out my nkisi. I had taken to carrying the god around with me since Mother had gone. I touched his head gently.

"You take that god wherever you go," Viola said, rolling her eyes. "Humans determine the course of their lives, not gods."

"Belief in a god is very important," I lectured. "Mother has taught me that."

Viola tossed her head. "Many good people who believe in God are punished for no reason. That should tell you that humans must take their lives into their own hands."

Casting my eyes away from her, I put the small god away. There was something wild and strange about my cousin today.

Viola took a deep breath and hied the horse on. "Do you know the recipe for pickled oysters?"

"No."

"Why not ask your nkisi?" she said with a gleam in her eye.

"You're being wicked," I scolded.

She laughed and shouted into the wind. "Mace, allspice, black pepper, and vinegar! That's what the recipe is!"

She made a sudden turn and urged the horse on toward the swamp.

"Is this the right direction to your house?" I asked, recognizing "the way to go out."

"We aren't going home," Viola's voice rang out. "We are going to town. We haven't any allspice in the kitchen."

"Why do we need allspice?" I asked. The horse was going quite fast. I gripped the seat to keep from falling.

"You heard the recipe," she said sharply. She cast a quick glance at me. "I didn't mean to snap at you," she apologized. "I'm nervous, that's all."

"About what?"

"About nothing," she replied, turning her eyes to the road. By the time we stopped in Hanover Square, my apron was covered with dust. Viola hopped down off the wagon and went into a shop, leaving me to hold the reins. Though the city bustled, I felt quite alone and somewhat frightened—especially when I remembered what Cousin D'Angola had said about pickpockets. Spying a small crowd gathering up the street, I stood up and strained to see what was going on. A woman with gray hair was in the stocks and people were jeering at her! One man even threw a stone. I sat down and tried to make myself smaller, clenching my hands in fear.

Viola returned with a small sack, which I took to be the allspice. "That's our excuse for coming to town," she said, jumping back into the driver's seat. Then she took a candy stick out of her pocket and stuck it into my hand. "There's also this."

"Thank you," I said nervously. "May we go?"

"Of course," said Viola. "But that sweet has a price. We are going somewhere else before we go home. And I must have your word that you won't tell my mother or father."

"Agreed," I said.

Viola seemed to know right where she was headed. We stopped

in front of a grand-looking red-brick house on Pearl Street and climbed down off the wagon.

"Where are we?" I asked.

"At the De Peysters'," Viola said. She smoothed her kerchief. "We'll knock at the side door."

"But why are we here?"

"To see Sampson."

"Won't your parents mind?" I asked.

"That's why you mustn't tell them," said Viola. She held my hands tight. "I have to see him sometimes, don't I? I cannot be apart from him all the time!"

Viola looked as if she might cry. Her behavior that day was so strange. One moment she was gleeful, then the next on the verge of tears.

"I won't tell anyone about your visit," I promised.

"I want you to come inside as well," she said, leading me to the door. "You never really got a chance to meet Sampson."

Viola knocked on the door. My stomach drew itself into a knot. What if Sampson himself did not answer, but the lord of the house? The one who owned Sampson? He might be angry with me and Viola for visiting!

Sampson's handsome face appeared through the glass. He opened the door.

"Viola!"

My cousin threw herself into his arms. Sampson was dressed all in blue. He hugged Viola tightly.

"You should not keep visiting me here," Sampson said. "There's no future in it."

"Don't say that," murmured Viola.

Sampson glanced over at me. "And who is this beautiful child you've brought with you?"

"My cousin," she explained, loosening her hold on him. She held out a hand to me. "Come, Monday, and meet Sampson."

Offering his own hand to me, Sampson took a few steps forward. "How do you do, Miss Monday?" He looked into my eyes and smiled. "I think that we have met before."

Sampson's smile had the warmth of sunshine. "I was at the Pinkster party."

"Oh, yes," said Sampson. "But you must live around here. For I know I've seen you."

"You can't have seen her," said Viola. "Monday lives far away in Africa. She's a world traveler."

"Ah! How very lucky you are," said Sampson.

Viola turned to me, beaming. "Didn't I tell you that Sampson was wonderful?"

Sampson grasped Viola's hand and gave it a squeeze. "Hush, you're embarrassing me."

"Well, can you invite me inside today?" my cousin asked. "Monday can tell you all about alligators."

"What are those?" asked Sampson.

"Cow-eating lizards," Viola explained.

Sampson gently took Viola's arm. "The family is out all day. Come in. Mother won't mind."

We followed Sampson through the door and into the foyer. At the far end on either side of a polished door were two identical red leather chairs that looked like thrones.

"Does a king live here?" I asked.

"Not a king, exactly," Sampson said quietly. "The man I work for owns ships."

"Sampson lives at the very top of the house," Viola said. "He has not shown me his room, but I'm sure that he can see all of New York."

"At home I have a house in a tree," I volunteered to Sampson. "Of course, it's only a house for me and my friend to play in."

Sampson smiled at me. "I'm sure I would prefer to live in your tree house than in my garret."

"Is your garret as fine as the rest of the house?" I asked, admiring the colorful hangings on the wall. I particularly liked one depicting a boy with wavy hair standing next to a dog.

Sampson chuckled. "Now that would be something—the master hanging tapestries in the butler's garret. No, my room is quite different from this part of the house. But I do wish I could show you the second floor. There's a large room built just to house tapestries, some even finer than those hanging here."

"The De Peysters have so much," Viola said, glancing wistfully at Sampson. "Why must they also have you?"

"They do not own my heart," he said quietly.

Sampson and Viola looked deeply into each other's eyes. I knew nothing about the feelings a man and woman could have for each other, but seeing Viola and Sampson in that moment, I felt that I knew what true love was. Sensing their need for privacy, I removed myself a few feet away, while Sampson and Viola embraced. Then, holding hands once more, they followed me.

"Would you like to sit in one of those chairs?" Sampson asked, pointing to the thrones at the end of the foyer. Viola smiled at me.

"I would," I replied.

"You, too," Sampson said, leading Viola.

Viola and I began giggling and ran down the corridor.

Sampson's face was beaming. "Please be seated, ladies," he said, directing us to the luxurious seats.

I sank down into one of the thrones and Viola sank into the other. We both laughed with delight.

"My rear has never known such comfort," Viola sang out mischievously.

Sampson surveyed us with a broad smile. "If only my poor master knew that two queens had come to call at his home today." He chuckled. "I have never cared for those chairs. The next time they need to be cleaned, I shall think of you two sitting there and smile."

"Who usually sits here?" I asked, wriggling against the stiff back of the chair.

"Certainly not I," said Sampson. "I have never taken a seat in any of these rooms."

We heard the creaking of a door and the sound of hurried footsteps. Sampson turned. There in the middle of the corridor staring at us was a beautiful little woman holding a large white bowl. Viola and I jumped up.

"What is the meaning of this?" she asked. Her voice was quiet but sharp.

"I asked them to sit, Mother," said Sampson. "There is no harm in it."

"There is harm in it, should the master come in," the woman responded.

"Good day, Dina," Viola said, bowing.

"Good day, Viola," the woman replied. Her face softened into a smile. She turned her eyes on me. "Is this your chaperon?"

"This is Monday, my cousin who is visiting."

The woman's eyes rested on me again. "How very nice to meet you. I am Sampson's mother, Dina."

I stared at the woman's face. I could not take my gaze from her eyes. They were very bright, just like Sampson's.

Sampson took the bowl from his mother and placed it on a sideboard. "Is this not the bowl you needed?" he asked.

"The mistress has changed her mind again," his mother replied. She pointed up to a shelf on the wall. "The mistress prefers the silver bowl for the trifle. Of course, the wedding is weeks away," Dina added, "which means she'll probably change her thinking several more times before then."

"I'll bring the silver one in for polishing," Sampson said, pulling a gleaming bowl down off the shelf.

During this conversation, Viola and I were standing quietly by, as if almost forgotten.

"I'm so sorry," Sampson said, turning to us suddenly. "The master's daughter is to be married early this summer. The wedding feast will be here."

"That will be a lot of work for you," Viola said, crossing to Dina.

"Nothing that I'm not used to," Sampson's mother said good-naturedly. She gave Viola a pensive look. "Do your parents know of your visit today?" she asked.

Viola lowered her eyes. "I'm sure they wouldn't mind. They have a great deal of respect for Sampson."

"I worry for the two of you," Dina said. She pressed Viola's hand, then turned away.

"Would you like to have some refreshment before you leave?" she asked, leading the way out of the foyer. "I have just made biscuits."

"That would be wonderful," Viola said, following her eagerly.

Carrying the gleaming bowl, Sampson brought up the rear with me. "And how are you enjoying your stay, Miss Monday?" he asked with a twinkle in his eyes.

"Very well," I replied. "Yesterday I went to Pinkster at Philipsburg."

Sampson's expression darkened. "I have many memories of that place. Pinkster was one of the better ones."

Beyond the corridor, there was a covered walkway that led out of doors to the back of the house. On the other side was the kitchen. The smell of baking greeted us. Sampson placed the silver bowl on the table and pulled up two wooden chairs.

"Please sit down," said Dina. She crossed to the hearth. The biscuits were on a board next to the oven, keeping warm.

"We'll have honey with them," Sampson said, taking a crock from a shelf.

"And give them some lemonade, too," Dina instructed. The two of them bustled around us, setting the table with blue and white saucers and cups. Two of the cups were cracked. Sampson made sure to give the ones that were not cracked to us.

Very soon the four of us were settled, eating the crisp biscuits smothered with honey and sipping sweet lemonade out of the cups. Sampson had poured the lemonade from a wooden pitcher. It was cool, and slices of fruit were floating on top.

"The biscuits are delicious," said Viola. "And so is the honey."

"My master has his own hives in the country," said Sampson.

"Of course it's Flip who really takes care of the bees," said Dina, passing the biscuit plate.

"Who is Flip?" asked Viola.

"Why, one of the master's people," Sampson murmured, turning away. "He's very knowledgeable."

An uncomfortable silence followed. I had almost forgotten that Sampson and his mother were slaves, but Sampson's comment had reminded me.

"So have you decided on the menu for the wedding feast?" Viola asked Dina, breaking the silence.

"The mistress will make that decision," Dina said, clearing her place. "But she has requested that I make the bride's cake in the same manner that I did for one of the Livingstons."

"Who are they?" I asked.

"Another family hereabouts," said Sampson. "They often hire Mother out from the De Peysters for special occasions."

"You're a very good cook," Viola volunteered, taking another biscuit. "I'm sure the cake will be wonderful."

"Lots of currants and almonds," Dina said. "That's the secret."

"I should like to have a bride's cake someday," Viola said in an envious voice.

Again the room became silent. A fly buzzed over my drink. Glancing sideways at Viola, I saw that her eyes were sad. Sampson looked downcast also. I looked up from my lemonade. Sampson's mother was staring at me. When I caught her eye, she did not look away.

"How bright your eyes are," she remarked.

I was startled. "I had thought the same thing about *your* eyes," I said shyly. "They are very much like Sampson's."

"So people have told me," Dina said.

I drained my cup and sucked on a lemon peel. From out of nowhere, our jolly refreshment had turned into something uncomfortable, as if the room were filled with things unsaid. There sat myself and Viola, free to come and go as we pleased, while Sampson and his mother were bound to the De Peysters. It was as though the difference in our conditions drove a wedge between us. And yet we were the same, and Viola and Sampson loved each other. Then with a pang I recollected the story Viola had shared about Sampson's mother—her baby girl had drowned while she tried to escape! I stared at the woman again as I recalled the child's name: Easter!

"Why are you staring so?" Viola said, jabbing me with her elbow.

"I'm sorry," I said, getting up quickly. Suddenly, my head was pounding with confusion. Easter was also the name of the child written about in Mother's book! What if the woman in the book and Sampson's mother should be one and the same? Dina had cleared the dishes and crossed to the counter. I stared at her back.

"Perhaps we should go," Viola said, standing. "I am supposed to be pickling oysters."

"It was so nice to see you again," Dina said. She crossed the room and took up the silver bowl. "Sampson will see you to the door. If I am to give this bowl a fine shine before the mistress returns, I must get started."

Sampson brushed Viola's arm. "I wish you did not have to leave," he said. "Monday has not told me about alligators yet."

"What are they?" Dina asked, smiling at me.

"Lizards who eat whole calves," I replied, staring. But my mind was not on the subject. I longed to know if she was the one who had done the writing, but who could I ask? My question would require so much explaining. Not only that, it would bring up the death of Easter—something I was sure Sampson and his mother would not want to discuss, it was so private.

"You are telling a falsehood, Monday," Dina said with a twinkle in her eye. "A lizard could not be so huge."

"They are in Madagascar," I replied.

"Surely you don't live there?" she said in surprise.

"Yes, she does," said Viola. "Her mother has brought her for a visit."

"Mother is a midwife," I blurted out quickly. "Her name is Leslie de Groot—do you know her?"

Dina's eyes grew wider. The silver bowl slipped out of her arms and fell to the floor with a crash. "Ah!" she cried, stooping to the floor. "The bowl is dented!"

"There, there, Mother," said Sampson, kneeling down next to her. "We can have the silversmith smooth it out."

"I'm sorry if I made you drop it," I ventured. Dina looked up. Her eyes bored through my own. Though I had noticed their brightness, I had not seen before the dark circles beneath them and the deep line that creased the center of her forehead. She kept her stare on me for an instant, as if taking in my whole being in one look. I turned my face away, only an instant later to reach instinctively for her hand as she struggled to stand up.

"Are you all right?" Viola asked, coming forward.

Dina nodded, still lightly holding my arm.

"Do you know my mother?" I asked again.

"No, I do not," replied Dina, withdrawing her hand from me. "Now I must ask you to leave and to not visit this house again."

"Neither of us?" Viola said, moving in closer. Tears sprang to her eyes.

Dina's eyes narrowed, as she focused on Viola. "A young woman traveling the streets alone is a dangerous thing. Do not come here again."

"Oh, please," begged Viola. "Sampson and I—"

"Do not be so harsh, Mother," Sampson pleaded.

Dina turned her back. "It is time that you should be going."

Viola bolted out through the back door and I ran with her. We did not stop running until we reached the wagon. With tears pouring from her eyes, Viola drove us quickly through the town. But by the time we reached the swamp, she had stopped crying.

"You are to tell no one of this," she said in a stern voice.

"Was I the one who made Sampson's mother angry?" I asked.

Viola ignored me.

"I'm sorry if it was me," I said. "I hope that you will be able to see Sampson again."

Viola clenched her jaw. "I cannot continue to live this way," she muttered.

"There's something I didn't tell you," I began to confess. "I found a book in Mother's box. I didn't show you, because I shouldn't have opened the box in the first place, and I had no way of knowing—"

"Be quiet," Viola said. "I am too upset to listen to your chatter."

"It isn't chatter," I protested.

"I have to think, Monday," she said sharply. "Please be quiet."

We got back and pickled oysters. Then two days later, Mother returned.

IN THE NAME OF GOD, AMEN. I, *James Phenix*, of Shawangunk, in Ulster County, yeoman, being sick. I leave to my daughter *Helena* my negro man "Tom," Also all that my dwelling house, barn, orchards and land thereto adjoining, lying between the Wallkill and the lane leading from Henry Van Weyens towards Burger Myndertse mill...

IN THE NAME OF GOD, AMEN. I, *Gerritt Van Bergen*, of Cattskill, in Albany County. I leave to my eldest son...the fall lying on the Catskill creek...also 1/2 of all my right and title to all the lands commonly known by the name of the Shingle Kill, ... Also my negro man "Anthony," and my negro man called "Jack," also my negro wench called "Gin," and my negro boy "John Taps..."

IN THE NAME OF GOD, AMEN. I, *Jeremiah Owen*, of New York, school master, being sick..."I give the clear income and rent of that part of my house and tenement adjoining the house of Mr. Varick, near the Broadway Market, to my executors for the use and benefit of Poor children in their schooling and instruction..."

From "Abstracts of Wills on File in the Surrogate's Office, City of New York, vol. V, 1754–1760."

Chapter Eight

"Mother! Mother!" I ran into her arms and she squeezed me tight. The hug she gave me was so big that I was nearly drowned in it.

"Frederick will be freed," she said, letting me loose. Her eyes glistened. "God has listened to my prayers. Oh, Monday! There is some justice in the world!" She grabbed me and hugged me again.

"Oh, Mother! That's wonderful!"

Holding me tight, she began to cry. In all my life, I had never seen my mother shed tears.

"You are not sad, are you?" I asked, patting her shoulder.

"My heart is bursting with joy," she said, wiping her eyes.

Cousin D'Angola and Cousin Pearl came into the study, followed by Viola and Werner.

"Paul has told me the good news," Cousin Pearl said. She touched Mother's hand. "I did not think you could persuade them."

"Leslie is a miracle worker!" Cousin D'Angola said, strutting across the study. "How did you do it, anyway?" he asked, stopping short.

Mother rose to her feet. "In Kingston I found lodging in a tavern. The owner's wife was expecting and it was her time."

"You delivered a baby?" I exclaimed.

Mother nodded.

"At such an inconvenient time," lamented Cousin Pearl. "After all, you were on a mission for Frederick."

"This birth had everything to do with my mission," Mother said brightly. "It turned out that the mother and I were related. She is my cousin Nancy de Groot, the daughter of my father's brother. She and her husband, Owen, run the tavern."

"That's luck," commented Cousin Pearl.

"You haven't heard even half," said Mother. "The child was a boy. His father, Owen, was so happy that he passed ale to all his customers."

"Get on to the part about Frederick," Cousin D'Angola prodded.

"I am coming to that," said Mother.

"Let her take her time," said Cousin Pearl.

Mother sat down and took in a breath. She did not usually talk so much. "One of Owen's chief customers is a justice of the peace. He was in the tavern on the day the baby was born," continued Mother. "Owen sent me to pour his ale and I introduced myself."

Cousin D'Angola's eyes popped out. "You poured ale in a tavern?"

Mother grinned. "That's not all I poured. Into the ear of that justice of the peace, I poured my brother's story."

"And that's how you did it?" Werner piped up from the corner.

Mother paused for a moment and looked up. "I cannot help but believe that the Lord was with me. For you see that justice of the peace remembered my father—he had purchased his barrels. And he also knew the Attorney General!"

"I understand the Attorney General has a country estate in those parts," Cousin D'Angola said.

"He does," said Mother. "He was there that very week, and through the justice of the peace, I received an audience."

A hush fell over the room.

"Is it possible, Leslie?" Cousin D'Angola ventured. "You and the Attorney General in the same room together?"

"It happened," said Mother. "He was a decent person. He heard Frederick's tale. I showed him the papers. And the justice of the peace had come with me to swear that our branch of the de Groots were free landowners. Though the Attorney General could not issue an actual writ, he has penned a letter in very strong terms to Kortwright, whom he knows quite well. When I deliver the letter, Frederick's freedom is guaranteed."

From the pouch she wore at her waist, Mother retrieved a document with a few lines of writing.

Werner and the family crowded around her to see. To think that a letter from one man to another held such power!

Cousin D'Angola embraced Mother. "God will reward you for all you have done for your brother."

Mother wiped away a tear. "It's not quite over, I'm afraid. I have to go collect Frederick. That means I will have to face Kortwright."

"I will go with you," said Cousin D'Angola. "And we'll take Anthony Portuguese with us and some of our other neighbors. We'll go in a contingent. Kortwright can't stand in our way. We have the law on our side."

Mother left the room with Cousin D'Angola, and Cousin Pearl followed them.

"Your uncle will be a happy man," said Werner. "Now he can go where he likes. No more watching over his back for the master."

"I have never seen my mother so joyful," I said.

"Some people are very lucky," said Viola, who had been sitting quietly in a corner. Taking a seat next to her, I said nothing. I knew that she was thinking of Sampson.

Several hours later, when it was already dark, Mother and Cousin D'Angola returned with my uncle. He was wearing a tattered hat, and his vest was frayed at the collar. All of his belongings fitted in one small bundle, which he carried slung over his back. Mother and Cousin D'Angola came in first and Uncle Frederick hung back by the doorway, as if he were waiting for something.

"Please come in," Cousin Pearl said, extending her hand to him. He peered into the room, wide eyed. "What is this heavenly place all full of color?" he asked, referring to Cousin Pearl's hangings.

"Our cousin is a weaver," said Mother. "Don't you remember?"

"There are probably a number of things I've forgotten," Uncle Frederick apologized. He smiled at Viola and Werner and me, then stood stiffly behind a chair.

"Sit, Frederick," said Cousin D'Angola. "You must be weary."

Uncle Frederick smiled sadly. "I'm afraid that is so. May I sit my weariness out at your table?"

"Of course," Mother said, rushing to his side.

Uncle Frederick sat down and took Mother's hand. "How can I ever thank you for what you have done?"

"You are my family," came her answer.

Cousin Pearl had waited supper for him. I had guessed that he would have been hungry, but after the first sip, he put down his soup-spoon.

"Do you remember that summer in our childhood, Frederick?" Cousin D'Angola said in a jolly voice. "When you and Leslie came to stay and we studied with the Reverend Huddleston?"

Frederick cracked a smile. "How could I forget *The English and Low-Dutch School-Master?*"

Mother chuckled. "I still have the copy we shared."

Cousin D'Angola tore off a piece of bread and dipped it into his soup. "Nice thing, learning. Imagine not knowing how to read."

Frederick sighed. "Imagine . . . Though for all the learning, I've not read much myself lately." His shoulders drooped.

"I am very grateful to you all," he said, "but I am not feeling as well as I might."

"Why not lie down then?" Mother suggested.

"Please take our room, Frederick," said Cousin Pearl.

"Yes, do," said Cousin D'Angola. "Leslie will show you where it is. I'll fetch you some cool barley water from the kitchen. That will help you rest better."

Mother walked with Uncle Frederick to the stairs. It was not that he was sick, exactly. Though weakened in some way, he could certainly walk on his own. But his enslavement had marked him, with a halting gait, bowed shoulders, an ugly brand on his neck, and the memory of a type of suffering the rest of us had never known.

"Your mother has promised me that we will go to Shingle Kill tomorrow, Monday," he said. He smiled at me over his shoulder. "I'll feel much better then."

"Don't you think you should wait a few days before traveling?" Cousin Pearl asked.

"My brother insists on going right away," said Mother. "I'll have to go with him to see that he gets settled."

"I'll tell you the names of all the trees and flowers if I can remember them, Monday," said Uncle Frederick.

Mother and her brother went upstairs. Soon after, Cousin D'Angola followed them with a cup of barley water.

"Five years of his life stolen," Cousin Pearl sighed, shaking her head.

"It isn't fair," Viola said angrily. "Kortwright should pay with five years of his own."

That night I hovered close to Mother in the study while she packed our things in the large leather bag. Ever since the night I had opened her wooden box, I had been haunted by the mystery I had found inside. Determined to know if the woman who had written about her life in the margins of the grammar book was indeed Sampson's mother, I told my own mother what I had done.

"While you were gone, I opened your box," I confessed.

She turned to me in surprise. "This box? . . . Ah, I left the key, didn't I? I had taken the papers belonging to Frederick and was in a hurry, I suppose."

She peered down at me. "So, what did you find inside?"

"Someone had written in a book," I said quietly.

She let out a breath. "And did you read the writing?"

"Yes," I replied. "Some poor woman had to say good-bye to her husband and children. I hope we never have to say good-bye like that," I added, gazing up at her.

"We won't," she said, touching my braids.

I let out a sigh of relief. Mother didn't seem angry. "So, who was it who wrote in the book?" I asked.

"An old friend of mine," said Mother. "Her name is Dina."

"I thought so," I exclaimed, "though she wouldn't admit it to me."

"What are you talking about?" Mother asked, sitting on the edge of the chair.

"Do you remember the young man who read the newspaper at the party? His name is Sampson."

"I remember him," said Mother. "What of it?"

"He is the son of your friend," I said. "He is the son of Dina."

Mother caught her breath ever so slightly. "I—I had no way of knowing. . . ." she stammered. "He had no other name. How do you know about him?" she demanded, standing up suddenly.

I shrank back. "He is Viola's friend. I went with her to the house where he is the butler. His mother works there as the cook. They are slaves."

"Ah!" said Mother. "What else?"

"Nothing else," I replied. "I asked Sampson's mother if she knew you, but she denied it."

"Of course she would," Mother said, looking away distractedly.

"Your friend has had a sad life," I said, coming closer to Mother. "Viola told me about how she accidentally caused her baby to drown—the girl named Easter. Were you the midwife who helped her when Easter was born?"

"Yes," Mother said softly. "I was." She hurried across the room and shut the door to the study. "Have you told anyone else about the writings?"

I shook my head. "I had wanted to tell Viola, but I became convinced that it would only make her sadder, if the story did turn out to be about Sampson's family. Viola is sad enough already. She's in love with Sampson, but they can't get married."

"I see," said Mother.

For a few moments, she paced. Then she spread her cloak out on the couch. "You will sleep with me tonight," she said.

"Thank you," I said. But I was no longer certain of her mood. "Are you angry with me?" I asked.

"No, I'm not angry," said Mother. "But you must promise not to tell anyone else about that story you read."

"All right," I promised, lying down on the bed. "Why is it that Dina said she didn't know you?"

Mother shrugged. "It's her choice. Did you tell her who you are?" she asked with a curious look on her face.

"Yes," I replied, yawning. "She became very upset when she found out I was from Madagascar. When I told her about alligators, she got so frightened that she dropped a bowl. The bowl got a dent. That made Dina angry. She said that Viola and I could not come back."

"No, you mustn't go there again," Mother said, stroking my back. She looked off into the distance. "Tomorrow we will go to Shingle Kill and help Uncle Frederick set up housekeeping. And then we'll go home."

Mother woke me before sunrise. Cousin D'Angola was to drive Mother, Uncle Frederick, and me to the river, where we would take a sloop to Kingston. From there we would take a smaller boat along the Wallkill River to the family farm at Shingle Kill. When we left, Viola, Cousin Pearl, and Werner were still sleeping.

"I will see you in a few days, Leslie," said Cousin D'Angola, waving good-bye to us. "Don't forget what you promised."

"I won't," she replied. "And you please do remember to look for notices regarding the departure of the *Peggy* and get word to Captain Boyd for me."

"I will," he said, waving his hat. "Good-bye, Monday! Take care, Frederick!"

Though the sun had hardly risen, there were lots of small boats on the river. The sloping shores were covered with trees. We sailed past farmhouses as well, surrounded by newly planted fields. After some hours had passed, we saw steep mountains with dense woods on one side and neat rows of fruit trees on the other side.

"There are tall trees and mountains at Shingle Kill," my uncle said, smiling up into the sun.

"I have promised Cousin D'Angola that we'll collect balm of Gilead from the fir trees," said Mother.

"Was that the promise you made him?" asked Uncle Frederick.

Mother nodded. "He has even sent me off with ox bladders to bring the stuff back in."

"What is balm of Gilead?" I asked. I liked the sound of that name.

"A balsam from trees that cures wounds of all kinds," Uncle Frederick explained. "I wonder if it cures aching bones."

Mother gazed at her brother. "How are you feeling today?" she asked.

"Numb," Frederick replied. "I had thought that should I be free again, I'd never stop dancing. But these years have aged me and I find that I'm hobbling."

"You will recover," said Mother.

He squeezed his sister's hand. "I know. You have given me the greatest gift, Leslie—you have given me back myself. It's only taken a day or two for me to realize that it's actually happened."

It was evening when we reached Kingston Landing, though there was still plenty of light. A boy my size standing next to a dugout canoe was doing a trick with a piece of rope. We stopped to watch him. First he knotted the rope and then motioned for me to test it. I stepped up and took a tug. The knot seemed secure. But with a sudden shake of his wrist, the boy made the knot slip out again. The captain of our sloop tossed him a coin.

"I am John Tapps," the boy said, stepping up to us. "I have my own ferryboat, which an Indian man helped me to build, and my master gives me leave to hire out. I can take you clear up into the mountains, if you say so."

"Perhaps we should stay the night with our cousins Nancy and Owen at their tavern and get a fresh start tomorrow. I don't know what we'll find at the farm. I did not have time to inspect it when I was here before."

"I will visit our cousins another day," said Uncle Frederick. "I want to go home."

My uncle reached into his pocket and put a coin into John Tapps's hand. "We are going west on the Wallkill," he said.

"Come aboard," said the boy.

We loaded our bags and got into the canoe. John Tapps paddled us away on a shimmering river, much smaller and less churning than the Hudson. In the early evening light, the trees were reflected on the river's surface. Fragrant yellow flowers lined the shore. And already there was a loud chorus of frogs.

"Do you see that tall cliff over yonder?" my uncle asked, pointing ahead on the right. "Stop at the pasture below it."

We beached the canoe next to the pasture and took up our bags.

"I'll be around if you need me again," the boy called. "Just ask for me at the landing."

"Thank you for your pains, John Tapps," my mother called back.

We crossed through tall grasses and then climbed a steep hill. The hill was overgrown with big trees.

"I see that Shingle Kill is in a jungle," I said.

"These are white oak and black walnut," said my uncle. "The leaves on the trees can become so thick that they blot out the sunlight."

"But on a hot day their coolness is welcome," my mother added.

A thorny bush caught my skirt as I trudged along the path. "Are we almost there?" I fretted. "My legs are becoming weak."

"That is because you have scarcely used your legs all day," my mother chided. "Try to keep up with us."

The trail became steeper. We saw a stack of huge rocks and two boulders that made the mouth of a cave. The cliff we had seen from the shore was to our left.

"Are there leopards here?" I asked, quickly skirting past the cave.

"There are black bears," my uncle said, "but they won't go out of their way to bother us. They are friendlier than some men I have met."

We arrived at a leveled-off place where the trees thinned out. A few steps more and we were in a bright clearing filled with tall yellow flowers. In the middle of the clearing there was a building partially hidden by overgrown grasses. Beyond that was a fresh green hill and beyond that the curve of mountains.

My mother shook her head. "Look at the house," she said sadly. She put her hand on my uncle's shoulder. "The earth has nearly swallowed it up."

But my uncle did not appear sad. Instead he began to walk ahead more quickly with his bag on his shoulder. My mother and I also picked up our pace. She had balanced the box on her head and was carrying our large leather bag stuffed with supplies. In one hand I had the sack and in the other my small wooden god. So this was Mother's childhood home! I began running.

By the time we reached the house, my uncle had thrown off his jacket and was pulling tall weeds out of the ground. The house, which was stone, was barely visible. Grasses, vines, and flowers had not only grown up all around it but also choked it from the inside out. Wild green things were sticking up out of the chimney and blocking up the windows. Branches poked through a hole in the roof. Pushing back the growth to take a look inside, we saw that a tree had taken root in the dirt floor. "What a pity!" I cried. It was as if the house had been imprisoned.

"We have our work cut out for us," my uncle said.

"We'll have something to eat," said Mother.

After a picnic of cold rice and chicken packed for us by Cousin Pearl, my uncle appeared refreshed. He took a small ax from his sack and began to cut away saplings while Mother and I took knives and cut a path through the tall grasses. The three of us worked until sunset. Then Mother made a small fire so that we could keep going. Using all our strength, we gradually unchoked the small house, pulling up by the roots the wild things that had taken it over. When we were done, the windows, door, and chimney were unclogged and only the tree in the center was remaining. The three of us stood back and surveyed our work. Tears streamed from Uncle Frederick's eyes. I too cried quietly. Our tears were for joy. We had freed the stone house of my family, which had survived neglect and the abuse of nature. Lit by the moon, the structure stared back at us proudly. We went inside, wrapped ourselves in blankets, and fell fast asleep in a corner.

When morning came, the house was filled with light. Uncle Frederick was still sound asleep, but through the front window I spied Mother outside, sweeping the yard with a branch.

"Good morning!" she called out to me. "There is bread on the hearth."

I hobbled over to the fire to get something to eat. The muscles in my legs and shoulders were sore. Warming my back at the fire and gobbling up Mother's good bread, I breathed in a deep draft of air.

"The air is very fresh here!" I said, peeking at her again through the broken panes.

Mother nodded. Outside the sun bounced off the mountain and the grass was carpeted with flowers. There was an unearthly beauty about this place.

Proceedings of the General Court of Assizes

*Robert Seary A Negro Man Being Indicted
and Arranged for Breaking Prison and Stealing
A Boate which with Others Runn Away with
out of the Mould or Harbour of this Citty on his
tryall Pleaded not Guilty Butt Being Found
Guilty by the Jury was Sentenced To be Tyed to
A Carts Arse and to Receive tenn Lashes or
Strips on the Bare back att Each Corner Round
the Citty And to be Branded in the forehead
with the Letter R.*

From "Proceedings of the General Court of Assizes," New York, 1680–1682.

Chapter Nine

That afternoon Uncle Frederick showed me how to catch partridge. The first thing he did was to make a square box out of some old clapboards. He then sprinkled some cornmeal on the ground and set the box over it, supporting it on one corner with a small stick. There was just enough room for a partridge to walk under. When the bird went after the corn, the small stick on the corner gave way, trapping the partridge beneath the box. As there seemed to be hundreds of these birds running through the field that day, Uncle Frederick and I caught more than enough.

Later on my mother joined us for a walk up into the woods where we found a stream. She went fishing with a hook Uncle Frederick had given her which was made out of a bird's claw.

"When I was a boy, an Onteora Indian taught me how to make that type of hook," he told me.

While my mother was fishing, Uncle Frederick pointed out a mockingbird to me and another bird called a robin redbreast. We also saw several gray hares and some huge black birds called maize-thieves. Then Mother caught a trout!

On the way back to the house, Uncle Frederick picked a bunch of tiny purple flowers and gave them to me. "These are called kalmia," he said. "And this," he added, plucking flowers from a sweet-smelling vine, "is honeysuckle." He bit the stem off one of the flowers and sucked it. He offered me one of the flowers. "Try it. It tastes quite sweet."

I bit the stem off and sucked the bottom of the blossom. A honey taste landed on my tongue. "Shingle Kill is a good place to be," I said. For no reason at all, Mother kissed me. The trout she'd caught flopped around in the bucket. Uncle Frederick let out a long sigh. Then he smiled and stretched his arms up to the sky.

Mother cleaned and cooked the fish. We ate and Uncle Frederick lay down to sleep. Mother sent me to gather kindling outdoors. Behind the house there was a lot filled with broken barrels. I scavenged the ground for pieces of wood that were not rotten. I returned to the house with a big bundle.

"Very good," said Mother.

"What next?" I asked. I was eager to make a home for Uncle Frederick.

"We'll have to repair the roof," Mother said, peeking up at a big hole. "But that will wait until after your uncle's nap. Why don't you and I go outdoors and sit?"

I followed Mother outside. We found a flat rock warmed by the sun to sit on.

Mother smiled gently at me. "I must speak with you about the writing you found in my box."

I bowed my head. "I'm sorry about all that. The key was there. I couldn't help myself. To be honest, I was hoping to find out something about my father."

Mother nodded. "I have not been very open with you about your beginnings."

"Who was my father?" I asked. "Won't you just tell me his name?"

"His name was Sampson," said Mother.

I smiled. "I like that name already. That's the name of Viola's friend."

Mother plucked a piece of grass. "He died of smallpox," she told me, "a year after you were born."

"In Madagascar?" I asked.

"No, here in America," said Mother. "You and I went alone to Madagascar, just as I told you."

"Why did we leave him?" I cried.

Mother sighed and turned away. "This will be difficult for you to understand. Your father isn't the only one we left here. You also had a brother."

My eyes smarted with tears. I felt shocked and betrayed. "I have a brother and you have not told me about him? You left him behind? For what reason?"

"He was not mine to take," Mother said. She stood up, wringing her hands. I had never seen her look so upset, not even when she had told me about Uncle Frederick.

"What is it, Mother?" I asked fearfully. "Did my brother die also?"

"No, your brother is alive," she said, turning to face me.

"Where is he then?" I demanded. "I have a right to know."

"I knew this would prove confusing," Mother said with a helpless look in her eyes. "I had planned to tell you about this much later. But now that you've met Dina, you must know the details of your early life."

"What does Sampson's mother have to do with all this?" I asked, reaching out for her. "Mother, please tell me. Where is my brother?"

"Dina's child did not drown, Monday," Mother said, sitting me down once more on the rock.

"Well, that is good news," I said. "But what has that to do with us?"

Mother swallowed. "Dina was your first mother," she said quietly. "Your brother, who is alive, is Sampson."

For a full moment I sat there. I could not take in what Mother was telling me. Suddenly, fear gripped me.

"You are my mother," I said, grabbing her hands. "You are the only mother I have."

Mother shook her head slowly. "Dina was your mother. I was the midwife."

"No!" I cried out. I took a deep breath. I felt as if I were drowning. Mother was the most important person in my life. "You brought me with you on the ship," I insisted. "You have raised me. I am your daughter!"

Mother hugged me tight. "Yes, you are my daughter. But you are Dina's daughter also. You are Monday, as you have always been. But once your name was Easter."

"The child who people think drowned? Did Dina try to kill me, then?"

"Of course not," Mother said, taking my shoulders. "Dina loved you. That is why she gave you to me. She wanted you to be free."

Tears fell out of my eyes in torrents. It was as if the ground on which I stood was giving way. I clung to Mother, trying to fathom what all this meant. I was Easter! And yet I wasn't. I knew that I was Monday. I was the daughter of Leslie de Groot. I was a free person.

"Does this mean that I am a slave?" I cried out.

"Hush," Mother said. "You are safe. Only three people in the world know your history—Dina, Uncle Frederick, and myself. 'Twas

Frederick who helped me in the first days that you and I were together before we left on the *Peggy*. It was also Uncle Frederick who brought me Dina's book that time he came to visit. She had sought him out to leave it with him. I suppose she meant for me to share it with you someday."

She patted my hand. "So now you know the truth."

I sat there, shivering with fear, trying to piece together the story. I saw Sampson's face and began sobbing all over again.

"Poor Sampson. He wants to marry Viola. Could you not have taken him also?"

"He was sold by that time," said Mother. "It was only through God's help that I was able to take you with me."

"Did you jump into the water and save me?" I asked.

Mother wiped my eyes. "No. It was your real mother's clever plan that brought it about. After her husband and son were sold, Dina was determined to take control of something in her life. Knowing that she might be separated from you one day, she gave you up of her own accord. She gave you up to me." Mother's voice broke with emotion. "I did not have a child. I promised to take care of you. Dina and I had known each other before you were born. One summer my parents sent me to New York and I went to a school for poor children and Africans. Dina had been brought to the city that summer by her master. She was learning to read. Dina did not abandon you to a total stranger. She thought I would be a good mother."

"And you are!" I cried, patting her arm. "But I still cannot make out what happened. Viola told me that Dina jumped into the water with her baby."

"When Mr. Hoglant's overseer came for her and the child, Dina made up an excuse to go back to the cottage," Mother explained. "I was waiting there. I'd already arranged my passage to Madagascar with Captain Boyd. When Dina returned to the dock, she was carrying a bundle. But the bundle wasn't a baby."

"What was it?"

"A loaf of hard bread wrapped tight in a blanket," said Mother. "Meanwhile, I took you in a cart on the back roads. Within a few days, we were on our way to Madagascar."

I tried to imagine the scene—Mother with me in a cart and Dina with the bread wrapped up tight.

"Was Dina trying to escape herself when she jumped into the water?" I asked.

"She jumped in full view of the overseer. She had no hope of escaping."

"Then why did she jump?" I asked.

"To protect you," said Mother. "When she got to New York, they would have discovered right away that she had not brought the baby. If people thought that the baby had been drowned, there would have been no questions."

"She could have drowned herself," I exclaimed.

Mother nodded. "Your mother was very brave. She risked her life for you."

I laid my head on Mother's lap and began to cry softly. "You were both brave," I murmured.

Mother stroked my head. "So now you know the whole story. You must not repeat it to anyone."

"Will they make me a slave again if someone finds out?" I asked.

"Someone might try," Mother said. She held me tighter. "But you mustn't worry. Shingle Kill is the safest place on earth. And soon we will be in Madagascar."

"Would I have belonged to Master De Peyster?" I asked, still sifting the details of the story.

"Mr. Hoglant was your original owner," said Mother. "You might have gone to De Peyster's with Dina or you might have been separated."

I shuddered. "It is lucky that she and Sampson are in the same place now."

Mother sighed. "That must be some comfort. How strange it must have been for her to see you at the De Peysters'. Her own child!"

"I think she liked me," I said, recollecting Dina's smile and the way she had rested her hand on my arm. The image brought fresh tears to my eyes. "Will I never see her again?"

"It would be too dangerous for you to go back there," said Mother.

I buried my head in her lap again. "I am so sorry for them," I cried. My poor mother! My poor brother! They were enslaved and so had my father been. My entire family, enslaved, and I had been spared.

During that evening's supper of partridge and rice, I sat lost in my own thoughts while Uncle Frederick and Mother spoke of the old times when they were children. Mother and I were wearing the yellow and orange dresses that we usually wore at home. Before we ate, Uncle Frederick said a blessing:

"Oh Lord, thank you for this bounty and for the riches of family. When the righteous are in authority, the people rejoice: but when the wicked beareth rule, the people mourn."

That night when I was alone, I prayed to my nkisi: "Thank you for letting that baby who fell into the water not be a baby at all, but a loaf of bread. Please protect Dina and Sampson and the new baby who was born on the *Peggy* and the women and men who went with the pirates. Let me prove by the actions of my life that I am worthy of my two brave mothers."

We stayed with Uncle Frederick for three more days. On our last afternoon, we climbed the mountain to gather balsam from balm of Gilead fir trees. There were thickets along the way and quite a number of fallen trees to step over. My uncle explained that they were young hickories, felled by the winter storms. At last we came to a jungle of towering silvery-colored trees. The boughs on some were so thick with needles that they leaned down and touched the ground. On the sides of their trunks were bulbous growths like blisters.

"What a find!" Uncle Frederick exclaimed. He was fighting his way through the growth with his ax, cutting a path for me and Mother. "I've heard that this balsam is becoming highly valued in Europe. Perhaps I should make a business of gathering it, instead of going back to making barrels."

"Here's a very large blister!" Mother said, stopping at a tree. Mother and Uncle Frederick each had with them bottles with sharp metal beaks on the end. She handed me a bottle. "Would you like to try it, Monday?"

I nodded. Mother showed me where to puncture the bulbous growth.

"Hold the bottle steady," she instructed. The metal beak had pierced the blister and a clear liquid was dripping out. When no more balsam seemed to be coming, I moved the bottle away.

"Smell it," Mother said.

I took a sniff and breathed in a strong, earthy fragrance.

"Remember that smell. That's balm of Gilead."

Uncle Frederick had also been gathering. Having punctured several blisters, his bottle was nearly half full.

"The Iroquois call this Cho-ko-tung," he said.

Mother crept behind him. "May I put some on your neck?"

Uncle Frederick nodded and loosened his shirt collar. Then with some of the balsam she had gathered, Mother gently touched the scar of my uncle's brand.

"I'm sorry to leave you so soon after your release, Frederick," Mother said.

"You must go," said Uncle Frederick. "Your ship may be leaving soon." He touched his neck gingerly. "With all this balm of Gilead on my doorstep, I'm sure that I'll be reborn." He turned to me with gleaming eyes. "And someday I'll come to visit you and see your lemur."

"As long as you are not wearing a blue cap," said Mother.

On our way back, Uncle Frederick suggested that I climb one of the tall trees. "I would do it myself," he said. "But I'm afraid I might not get down again."

"May I?" I asked Mother, hiking my skirt up.

"Of course," she answered. "There is probably a wonderful view from there."

I shinnied up the trunk and climbed out on one of the limbs. The evenly spaced branches of the tree created a ladder, and the thatch at the top was almost as thick as a roof. Holding on to a branch, I nestled in the arms of the tree and looked down at the earth. I saw the farm at Shingle Kill, which we had rescued from the overgrowth. I could also see the path leading down to the river. And beyond the river, there was a tumbling waterfall!

"What do you see?" Uncle Frederick cried out from below.

"A beautiful waterfall!" I called down to him.

"I thought as much!" he shouted. "That is the same view I kept in my heart all those years I was away. Do not forget it, Monday!"

I peered down. The waterfall was not my only view. There was also the picture of my mother standing with Uncle Frederick, both of them looking very small and holding hands. I tucked the picture away in my memory along with the waterfall.

The following day, my uncle walked with us to the river with our bags. After less than an hour's wait, we saw a small boat. It was John Tapps, the ferryman we'd met on the way up.

"Hello, John Tapps," Uncle Frederick called. "Have you any rope tricks today?"

"I would settle for a ride to Kingston Landing," Mother chimed in.

"At your service," said the boy, paddling toward shore.

Mother turned to Uncle Frederick. "You will always be in our thoughts."

Mother's brother kissed her cheek. Then he lifted me a few inches up off the ground. "I am too big to be lifted," I protested.

"I am only testing my strength," joked Uncle Frederick, giving me a big hug. "You are a strong girl, Monday. Do not forget me, and have a safe voyage."

I hugged Uncle Frederick back with the biggest hug I had. "Be well, Uncle," I said.

"Will we never see him again?" I asked as John Tapps paddled us away.

"We do not know what the future holds," Mother said quietly, "but the distance is very great between our two homes."

On the way back to New York, the river churned wildly. Mother and I stood at a safe distance from the deck rail of the sloop.

"Before he was sold, your father was the boatman at a manor called Philipsburg," Mother said, staring out at the waves. "I did not know him well, but I do know that he was highly respected. He was also very proud when you were born."

I tried to imagine my father's face. If only I could have known him! "I was at Philipsburg myself," I told Mother. "Our cousins took me for Pinkster. I saw a play about Cuffee and I met an ancient man named Charles."

Mother's face lit up. "I also met an elderly Charles there. Is he still living?"

"He still lives," I said. "He called me Dina."

"You do look like her," said Mother.

The new wound inside me smarted. "Then I must look like my brother as well," I murmured. To think that I had a mother and brother I had only just discovered and was about to leave them.

When we got to New York, we hired a cart and driver at the dock. The driver took us bumping across the swamp to the D'Angolas'. I jumped down and ran to the house. How I had missed Viola!

Cousin D'Angola opened the door. His face was drawn. "What's happened?" Mother asked.

"I thought you might be my daughter coming home," he said with a sigh.

Turning back inside, he left open the door. Cousin Pearl was kneeling on the floor, her face turned up to the god on the mantel.

"Where is Viola?" I asked, bursting into the room.

"Missing," said Cousin D'Angola, "since yesterday. We have looked for her everywhere."

"Ah, cousins!" said Mother.

"And we have just received word that Sampson has run away from the De Peysters. A soldier was here asking if we had seen him. De Peyster has offered a large reward for his return."

"Sampson has run away?" I darted toward the door to look out. "They must be together then."

Cousin Pearl caught me by the arm. "If you know something about this, you must tell us. They need our help."

"I don't know anything, I promise," I cried, wiggling out of her grasp, "only that Viola and Sampson love each other."

"I should never have invited him to this house," Cousin D'Angola growled.

"We guessed that Viola had feelings for him," Cousin Pearl said softly. "But no one thought she would be foolish enough to act on them."

"Viola is a child," said Cousin D'Angola. "I will never forgive Sampson for putting her in danger. By doing so, he has betrayed me."

"Perhaps they are not together," Mother suggested.

"We can hope that," said Cousin Pearl.

"Or if they are together, perhaps they'll come here," Mother said in a comforting voice.

"Viola knows all too well that I would not let her run away with Sampson," said Cousin D'Angola. "He is not a free man."

"We'll have to look for them," said Mother.

"I have looked," said Cousin D'Angola, "but I will search again."

"Do you know anyone who might be sympathetic to Sampson's cause, cousin?" Mother asked.

"There are people in Nyack who might help him get away. I'll send word through the Portuguese family. They're part of the network. I have great respect for Sampson. I will do what I can to help him escape," Cousin D'Angola said. "But mark my words, if Sampson does make a run for his freedom, Viola will not go with him. My daughter will not live the life of a runaway."

"I pray that no one knows yet of her involvement in Sampson's escape," Cousin Pearl murmured. "The punishment for aiding the escape of a slave can be severe. As for Sampson, his master has the power to put him to death."

Mother came close and squeezed my hand.

Alone in Viola's room that night, I sat up on the mattress made of corn husks. My mind was filled with thoughts of Viola and Sampson. Viola had taken steps to be with the person she loved! And my brother had run away from slavery—he would be free like Uncle Frederick and myself! Like Mother's mother, Mando, he had walked out of his wooden shoes! Tiptoeing across the room, I pressed my face to the window. The tree in front of the house made a shadow on the yard in the moonlight. Then from behind I heard a soft scratching at my door. I quickly went to open it. Werner stood there holding a lantern. His red hair was loose and he was wearing a long nightshirt and boots.

"Come—" he whispered, motioning me out the door. "Your cousin . . ."

I followed him down the hall to the stairs. Though he did his best to creep, his boots still made a slight clumping.

"Is that you again, Werner?" Cousin Pearl's voice rang out.

"Yes," the boy called. "Going to the privy again."

We stood still for a bit, listening for Cousin Pearl to turn over. When everything was again still in the house, we crept down the stairs. Werner passed the study first, making sure that Mother had not been disturbed, then motioned for me to follow. We slipped out of the house.

"Where is she?" I whispered.

Werner pointed to the kitchen. We ran across the yard and ducked inside the dark building. I did not see Viola at first. Then she stepped away from a wall. I hugged her.

"Oh, cousin!" she whispered. "I could not leave without saying good-bye to you. When this whole thing is through, tell my parents that I love them."

"I will," I promised, wiping away a tear. "Where is Sampson?"

"Hiding in the cripplebush." Using Werner's lantern to see by, she took bread and dried beef from the larder and thrust it into a sack she had with her.

"Your father is going to try to help him escape," I said, keeping close to her elbow.

"Where is Father now?"

"Went out looking for you," said Werner, "and he hasn't come back."

"I must hurry then," Viola said, clutching the food sack. "He mustn't find Sampson."

"But he's going to help Sampson," I said. "The Portuguese family will help him get away."

Viola's eyes flashed. "Will they help both of us?"

"Your father said he didn't want you to go," I admitted.

"I didn't think so," said Viola, turning to the door. Suddenly we heard the soft breaking of twigs on the path. Viola ducked under the table and Werner crept closer to the wall. A shadowy figure slipped through the doorway. In the moonlight, I recognized Sampson.

"Are you there, Viola?" he whispered.

"Yes, my love!" she called softly. Creeping out from beneath the table, she ran to his side.

"You shouldn't be here," she warned.

"I was worried about you," he said.

"Both of you better go back to the cripplebush," Werner said nervously. He came forward with the lantern.

"Hello, good Werner," said Sampson, giving Werner a pat on his shoulder. "Has Viola told you the plan?"

"Yes," Werner said grimly. "I'll meet you with the wagon in the morning."

Viola and Sampson turned to go. I reached out of the shadows and touched Sampson's shirtsleeve. He turned back, startled.

"Monday . . . why are you here?"

"I asked her to come," Viola said hastily. "When we are gone, she will take my message of love to Mother and Father."

"You are a sweet child," Sampson said, touching my head lightly. "Have a good life. We must go now."

"Wait!" I said, grabbing his hand. He looked at me with a puzzled expression. My heart was pounding. "I must say something before you go."

Sampson tried to pull his hand away, but I held tight to him.

"For heaven's sake, cousin—" Viola hissed. "Let him go."

"I can't," I cried. "Not before I tell him."

Sampson's face softened. He came closer to me. I was trying very hard not to cry. I was saying hello and good-bye to my brother in the same instant.

"I . . . I am your sister." My words came out haltingly. "I am Easter." He knelt down and put his arms on my shoulders.

"What is that you've said?" he whispered.

"She did not die," I told him. "The body in the water was a loaf of bread. Your mother gave your sister away to the midwife. To my mother Leslie. I am Easter. I am she."

Sampson stared at me, incredulous. Then I felt his arms around me, trembling with feeling. "I knew in my heart that my mother could not have done that. I have always hoped. . ." He kissed my cheek. "Mother was upset for days after your visit. I thought it was because of Viola." He hugged me again. "You are risen from the dead. My sister!"

"What amazing news, cousin," Viola said in a distracted voice. "I cannot quite take it in."

Werner tapped Sampson's shoulder. "The doctor might be returning. You must go."

"Werner is right," Viola said, placing a hand on Sampson's shoulder. My brother stood up and smiled at me.

"We will meet again. I promise."

They darted out into the darkness, carrying the sack. A cold fear went through me. "Will they sleep in the swamp?"

"They have a good hole to hide in," Werner replied. He felt for my hand. "Let's go back to the house."

I went along with him, treading the path carefully.

"I want to go with you tomorrow," I whispered to Werner.

"It will be dangerous," he answered quietly.

"The three of you might need me," I insisted, my desire to help my brother overcoming my fears.

"We might need someone to be a lookout," Werner admitted.

"First thing in the morning, I will make a delivery for Mrs. D'Angola. I'll be driving the wagon. Meet me at the end of the road."

When I finally fell asleep that night, I had a terrible dream: Mother and I were leaving. No one was at home but Cousin Pearl. We said good-bye to her, but she did not answer. Her eyes were frozen in grief, but her hands moved like water over her loom. She was weaving another shroud. In the wagon, Mother and I rode through the town. A crowd had gathered. The horse came to a stop. A boy had been put in the stocks. His head was shaved. I recognized him as Werner, having lost his red hair! There was a girl standing next to him—Viola! She was very thin. Her favorite pink kerchief lay torn on the ground next to the shell bracelet, which was shattered. Viola was weeping. Cousin D'Angola stood near with his hands tied behind him. And next to him, my brother, naked to the waist, his arms tied to a post. A man in a powdered wig raised a cat-o'-nine-tails and brought it down upon Sampson's back! The crowd cheered. My brother flinched, but did not cry out. I started screaming. . . .

Run-Away from *Richard Harris* of Staten Island, a Negro named Tom, speaks good English. About 30 years of age. Run-away at the same time, a Negro boy named Harry, 14 years old, has an impediment in his speech, speaks good French and has lost one of his foreteeth: They both had light coloured kersey jackets with white flowered mettal buttons: Harry had a cap on such as marines generally wear, and Tom had a great-coat with a cap to it that covers his head on occasion.

From the *New York Mercury Gazette*, January 15, 1759.

Chapter Ten

At the first sound of birds, I was awake. The grownups were moving about downstairs. Stealing out into the hallway, I listened.

"I am going to New Harlem," Cousin D'Angola announced. "Anthony Portuguese has heard rumors of a young couple in hiding there. He is meeting me at the end of the road with his horse and cart."

"Would you like for me to go with you, cousin?" Mother's voice rang out.

"Yes," I heard Cousin D'Angola reply. "I mean to persuade Sampson to let Viola come back home with me. I may need your help."

I heard their footsteps and then the front door creaked open. I peeked down the stairway. Mother glanced up and caught my eye.

"Awake already? Perhaps you should take more rest."

"I am fine, Mother," I said.

She smiled up at me. "I will be back as soon as I can. Stay close to the house and obey your cousin Pearl."

"Yes, Mother."

At breakfast, Werner and I sat alone while Cousin Pearl sat staring at the window.

"Is the delivery ready?" Werner asked. I saw him stuff two biscuits in his pocket.

"On the front table," Cousin Pearl said, not taking her eyes from the window.

Wiping his hands on his breeches, Werner crossed the room to the table by the door. Lying in sumptuous folds were two linen shrouds, one brown and the other a violet color. He picked them up. I popped up from my seat and ran to the door.

"Where are you going?" asked Cousin Pearl.

"To milk Swan," I replied.

"Very good," said Cousin Pearl, keeping her gaze out front. "You know where to go, Werner," she muttered. "The Reverend is expecting the delivery."

"Very good, Mrs. D'Angola," the boy said, sticking his hat on.

We ducked out the door. "I will be waiting," Werner whispered. He went to hitch the horse to the wagon and I went into the stable. I spoke with Swan and made a loud noise with the bucket. When Werner passed with the wagon, I ducked out and hid behind the stable. Then I darted across and ran behind the house. Still at her post at the front window, Cousin Pearl didn't see me. But I could see the wagon waiting at the end of the road. Lifting my skirts, I ran through the high grasses. Werner offered me a hand and I took it, jumping aboard. I picked the shrouds up off the seat and laid them in my lap. Werner urged the horse toward the swamp.

"Why did they hide so close to home?" I asked.

"It's a good place," said Werner. "Only a few people know their way around there. Some soldiers were looking for Sampson yesterday and marched right by them."

"A wonder that Cousin D'Angola did not discover them," I said.

"He didn't look very thoroughly here," Werner explained. "He expects them to be running, not waiting in one place."

At a narrow part of the swamp, Werner pulled up on the horse. The road was only a thin line at this point, overgrown by reeds as tall as my mother.

"Where are they?" I whispered. "I don't see them."

Werner pointed to a half-fallen swamp tree. Where the front of the tree had once dug in its roots was a dark hole. He pointed and then whistled softly. Sampson's head poked out and then Viola's.

Sampson hoisted himself out, then reached for Viola. They were both covered with mud.

"Thank you, Werner," Sampson said, blinking into the sunlight. He glanced at me in alarm. "You should not be here, sister."

"I want to help you," I said.

"Please go home," Viola pleaded.

"You cannot stop me," I insisted.

Werner had dumped the shrouds into the back of the wagon. He was spreading one of them out. "Hurry!" he said. Sampson and Viola ran to the back of the wagon and Sampson helped her on. "Go look out," Werner said, waving me up the road. "Whistle if someone is coming, then hide yourself in the grass."

I ran back and forth up the road. Sampson was wrapping Viola in one of the shrouds.

"What are you doing?" I asked.

"We are going to be dead," Sampson muttered.

"Do not say that," I begged.

He smiled over his shoulder. "We will not die. We are only on our way to a different life. I know the captain on a sloop called the *Crispus*. He will smuggle our 'bodies' to Philadelphia. There's work to be had in Philadelphia. We can blend in there."

Viola lay in the wagon, wrapped in the violet shroud from head to foot.

"Can you breathe?" Sampson asked, leaving a space near her nose.

"Yes," came her muffled reply. "Hurry, my love!"

Werner climbed in next to her and began to spread out the second shroud. I grabbed the other end to help him. We wrapped my brother in the earth-colored fabric.

"Thank you, Monday," Sampson whispered. "Now you must go home."

"Not until you are safe on board the *Crispus*," I vowed.

I jumped aboard next to Werner, who was now in the driver's seat. "Where are we going?"

"To the graveyard," said Werner. "The captain of the *Crispus* will be waiting in a tavern just up the street from there. When I go inside to fetch him, you'll stay with the wagon."

In the back of the wagon, Viola and Sampson kept very still. One could almost have believed that they were corpses.

"Are you sure you want to keep going?" Werner asked. "No telling what punishment they'll mete out if we're caught."

"You would be punished as well," I pointed out.

Werner tugged on his cap. "I know what it's like to be on the run," he said. "My parents were in service. When they got scalped, the owner of the farm where we lived wanted me to work out their indenture. They each had five years left. That would have meant ten years' labor without pay for me. So one day I ran. Dr. D'Angola took me in and gave me a job. So I owe them."

"But my cousin D'Angola doesn't approve of Viola's running away," I reminded him.

Werner shrugged. "He wouldn't be able to stop her. Somebody might as well help."

My body began to shake with fear. We were entering the city. The street near the meal market seemed unusually empty. Then I smelled smoke. As we drew closer to the harbor, we began to see more people. Some of them were running. Two wagons drawn by white horses and filled with men raced past us.

"Someone has set a fire," Werner said.

I gazed up ahead. A black cloud was over the river.

"What is burning?" I asked worriedly.

"Maybe a warehouse," said Werner, "or a ship. It's lucky. If there is a fire, no one will be paying attention to us."

He pulled up in front of the African graveyard. Up ahead on the other side of the street was the Sign of Two Cocks Fighting, the tavern where we had stopped with Cousin D'Angola.

"If anyone questions you, tell them that you are waiting for the gravedigger," the boy said, slipping down to the ground. "I am going to get the captain of the *Crispus* at the tavern."

For what seemed like a very long time, I sat there with the bodies of my cousin and brother. The street was deserted, and ashes from the fire sifted through the air. Beads of sweat popped out on my forehead. I glanced back at the lifeless-looking shrouds. I put my hand in my pocket to touch my nkisi and realized in a panic that I had forgotten it. There was no one at all to help me!

The heat bore down on my head and the smoke from the fire made my eyes water. I stared at Viola and Sampson—surely they were even more parched than I was! I worried that they had stopped breathing.

"Are you all right?" I whispered.

"Yes," they murmured softly.

I gazed up the street. There was no sign of Werner. "Where is he?" I muttered out loud.

Suddenly, I felt a hand on me.

"Monday?—"

I turned in shock. Captain Boyd stared up at my face.

"Why are you here?" he asked. "Where is your mother?"

"She is. . . she is not with me," I stammered.

"What are these bundles in the back of the wagon?" he asked, staring at Viola and Sampson. "They look . . . like corpses." He turned to me with a question in his eye.

"They are bodies," I said. "I am waiting for the gravedigger."

"Alone?"

"My . . . my mother has gone to fetch him," I lied.

Captain Boyd took off his hat. "I am so sorry. Are these relations?"

"Yes," I replied, barely able to catch my breath. My mind whirled. I had to get rid of Captain Boyd somehow. Any minute Werner might be coming with the captain of the *Crispus*.

"I am very thirsty," I said, turning to him. "Do you know where there is any water?"

"You cannot drink the water here," said Captain Boyd. "Would you like to come with me to the tavern? There's a cool punch there."

"No, thank you," I said, "but perhaps you might go get me some."

"I will wait for your mother," he said. "I won't leave you alone."

The captain stared at me intently. Sweat poured off my brow.

Not knowing what else to do, I lifted the reins to the horse. "On second thought, I'll . . . I'll drive on. My mother is meeting me at the harbor."

"You have told me that she is meeting you here," he said, lifting an eyebrow. "And where else would you go with these bodies? Are they not ready for burial?"

"I must meet Mother anyway," I blurted out, struggling to regain my composure. "I beg you. Please let me go."

"I will go with you," Captain Boyd said, putting a firm hand on my arm.

I jerked away and the horse lurched forward. "I must go alone," I cried.

He jumped up onto the wagon seat and grabbed the reins. "You are hiding something from me," he said, boring his eyes into mine. "Tell me what it is. Perhaps I can help you."

"You cannot help with this," I said in a faltering voice. A slight stir came from the back and my eyes flitted for an instant to the shrouds. The captain's gaze followed my own.

"Did someone ask you to do something you shouldn't?" Captain Boyd demanded in a harsher tone. "One of these relatives you've met here?"

"No!" I cried.

"You are lying to me," said the captain. "What is in the back of the wagon? You and I both heard something stir!"

Sampson sat up and gave his head a toss. The top part of the shroud fell off, revealing his face. Captain Boyd reached back and grabbed his throat.

Struggling to untangle his arms from the shroud, my brother wrested the captain's hands from around his neck.

"Leave the girl alone!" Sampson cried. "She has no part in this!"

"Who are you?" the captain demanded. "You're a runaway, aren't you?"

"Yes," Sampson said. He jumped off the wagon and stared up defiantly. "I belong to the house of De Peyster."

A soft moan came from Viola. She lurched up and threw the cloth from her face. "Run, Sampson!" she cried.

But Sampson continued to stand there.

"And here's another one," Captain Boyd snarled.

"She is a free woman," Sampson explained.

"She is my cousin Viola," I pleaded. "Don't hurt her."

"Monday and Viola are blameless," Sampson said, coming forward. "Please take me back to my master. But spare them any punishment."

Captain Boyd curled his lip. On the other side of the road, a woman had stopped to peer at us.

"Get in!" the captain snapped.

"Why should he?" Viola challenged.

"Do as I say," he hissed, "or all three of you will be tied to a whipping post."

Sampson got back in and lay down. We took off together down the road, with the woman staring after us.

"Where are we going?" I asked, my heart pounding in fear.

"Somewhere private," Captain Boyd said. "To think those two would use an innocent child to help out their scheme. I'll turn them in, all right. But I won't have your life ruined."

"Did they threaten you?" he asked, glancing over at me. "I'm sure that your mother has no part in this."

"Mother does not know," I admitted. "And no one threatened me."

"You don't have to cover up for them, Monday," he said, urging the horse down an alley.

The wagon stopped near a deserted slip. I could see a boat burning out on the river.

"The *Crispus*," the captain announced in an offhand way. "She caught fire this morning while her captain was in the tavern. Now he's trying to put out the fire, poor fellow."

My heart sank. Things could not have been worse. Not only had we managed to land in Captain Boyd's hands, the very boat that would have taken Viola and Sampson to freedom was on fire.

"Get down," Captain Boyd ordered, giving me a nudge. I jumped off the wagon and hurried to my brother and cousin, who were climbing down off the back.

"Run!" I whispered, giving Sampson a shove. But he and Viola did not take the chance.

"We would not leave you, Monday," said my brother.

The three of us faced the captain, who had taken out his pistol.

"Don't try anything," he said, waving the gun in Sampson's face.

"I have already surrendered, sir," Sampson said. "But please let Viola and Monday go home."

"I certainly would not have the child punished," he responded in a surly voice. "I suppose you two are a couple," he said. "An ignorant choice for a free young woman."

"I love him," Viola said.

Captain Boyd glared. "By law you and Monday should also be put on trial. But I cannot do that to Leslie de Groot's daughter. I have known her too well and for too many years."

"You do not know her!" my voice rang out.

"If I were you, I would not be so insolent," Captain Boyd said with a scowl.

"You do not know her," I repeated, summoning my courage more.

"Don't talk nonsense," he said, dismissing me. "I am your only friend in this affair."

"You are not my friend," I said, staring him in the eye.

"Don't make things more difficult, Monday," the captain said, stepping toward me. "I will take this man back to his master. No one will know of your involvement. I will even go easy on your cousin," he added begrudgingly. He stretched out his hand. "Now come and get into the wagon."

"Save yourself, Monday," urged Sampson.

My legs stood their ground, though my insides trembled with the knowledge of what I had to do.

"If you take Sampson to De Peyster, you must take me also," I declared. "Because I too am a runaway."

"What? . . ." he stepped back.

"Please don't, Monday!" Sampson exclaimed. "Don't risk your own safety."

"What is this about?" Captain Boyd demanded, glancing back and forth among the three of us.

"You are going to take Sampson back to his master to be punished," I said.

"He is property," stated Captain Boyd.

"He is a person!" I protested. "And he is also my brother!"

"You're talking nonsense," he said. "They've worked a spell on you. A slave is not a person!" he cried shrilly. "A slave is a thing. You are someone I know! I know your mother!"

"He is my blood brother, I tell you—" I cried. "I am a runaway. My mother took me to freedom on your ship."

"On m-my ship?" he stuttered. "But I trusted her."

Sampson put an arm around my shoulder. "Ah, sister," he moaned. "What have you done to yourself?"

"Only what you would have done," I said.

"What all of us should do if we have the choice to make," Viola said, weeping.

The captain's arms dropped to his sides. "This man legally belongs to De Peyster," he said in a bewildered voice. "It is the way of our world. The way the world thinks."

"We do not all think that way," Viola said fervently.

"I do," the captain growled, "and that is something that I cannot change."

"Then you are a slave," I spat out.

Captain Boyd looked stung. "What did you say to me?"

"You are a slave," I said. "A slave to your thinking. If you have not the power to change it, to see the wrong in it, then you are as enslaved as my brother."

I stood between Viola and Sampson, holding fast to their hands.

"We are ready," Viola said quietly. "Where Sampson goes, we go also."

The captain slowly put his pistol in his belt and stared. In his wizened face, I saw reflected the face of a younger man who had been different. He silently raised a hand to his eyes, as if removing a cinder.

For London
THE SHIP EDWARD,
WILLIAM DAVIS, COMMANDER

will sail with all good speed (Having 2/3 of her cargo engaged) has good accomodations for passengers...

From the *New York Mercury Gazette*, April 30, 1759.

Chapter Eleven

The three of them stood on the shore in a line: Cousin Pearl, Cousin D'Angola, and Werner. Mother and I stood at the stern, waving until we could no longer see them. The ship cut a restless path across the bright river. We were going out the same way we had come in. Only I was a different person. I was no longer plain Monday but *Easter* Monday. Staring into the choppy water, I thought of Dina, the mother who had borne me. I had not had a chance to see her again. I folded the image of her bright eyes in my heart along with the memory of Uncle Frederick and the waterfall. Mother and I circled the deck. Boats passed going into New York. Only when the river had been left behind did we open our cabin. There in a far corner beneath the portal were Viola and Sampson.

"It's safe to come out now," Mother said, touching Viola gently.

I offered Sampson my hand. "Come outdoors and take the air," I said.

My brother stretched up and smiled.

Viola wiped away a tear. "Did Mother and Father send me a message?"

Mother hugged my cousin close. "They send their blessing and all their love. They also sent this," she added, pressing a small purse into Viola's hand.

"And this as well," I said. I handed Viola a folded piece of woven cloth which I had been holding. It was the color of a morning sky— pale blue, streaked with pink. "Your mother sends it to you for your wedding dress." Viola hugged the cloth to her chest.

"Werner also asks to be remembered," I said.

"He has been a true friend," said Viola. "I cannot quite believe that this has all happened. That Sampson is free and that we will be married."

"Believe it," Mother said. She extended a hand to Sampson. "Shall we go out on deck?"

We walked outside. The sea was a brilliant turquoise and the air was delicious.

"A wonder that a man like Captain Boyd would offer to help us," said Sampson, gazing up at the clouds.

"Who can plumb the depths of one person's heart?" Mother replied. "It seems that the captain was ripe for a conversion. He only needed Monday to call on his conscience. On his next voyage there will be no people in the hold."

Reaching into my pocket, I walked to the rail and threw my nkisi overboard.

"Do not throw away your god!" Viola protested.

I watched the wooden god tumble into the waves.

"I do not throw him away," I said. "I only send him back to comfort our family. To comfort them until we return."

The ship was advancing. The four of us stood in a line looking out at the ocean before us.

Author's Note

I love rivers. The river of my childhood in Washington, D.C., was the Potomac. And my summers in Virginia were spent swimming in a little squirt of a thing called the Hazel. But after I moved to the New York vicinity, my favorite river became the Hudson. Touring the old mansions in the Hudson River Valley with my husband and daughter, I was enthralled by the views and impressed by the sense of history in the region. As a person who spends most of her time imagining, I found myself wondering what it would have been like to live in the area two hundred and fifty years ago, just before the Revolution. The river would have looked different, because the trees that frame the view would have been different. The people, of course, would have looked different too, I thought, conjuring images of the Dutch and the colonial British. But what about the African Americans? I asked myself. What might a person like myself have been doing on the banks of the Hudson? Perhaps I wouldn't have been there at all—it wasn't until quite recently that I'd heard much about an African presence in colonial New York, and one does not usually associate the North with slavery. But I stubbornly continued to try to imagine myself there. Would I have been enslaved, I wondered. Or a free person? Would I have known how to read? Who would my family and friends have been?

In this frame of mind, I made a trip to Philipsburg Manor in Tarrytown, New York. I had heard about a community of enslaved Africans who had run a successful mill there in the eighteenth century. For several days, I sat poring over records in the library. I was most struck by an inventory of goods taken after the death of the owner of the manor. Along with silver tankards, sheep, and spinning wheels were listed the names of twenty-three African people. By all accounts they had lived together for many years and run the mill, while their owner lived in New York City. Also noted in the inventory was a payment rendered to a midwife to aid one of the "Negro women" in her recovery. Just after the owner's death, a baby had been born! Also in the file was a copy of a newspaper advertisement, dated April 1750, announcing the auction of the entire slave community. I stared at the names, trying to imagine what the people must have been feeling, knowing that they would be sold. I thought of that mother and her new baby, and a story began to materialize.

I spent the next several months in libraries, reading old newspapers and ship logs, scanning wills for the names of people left as property. I learned that there had been lots of runaways, some of whom were described as highly skilled and articulate in various languages. I also began to read about the free black population in eighteenth-century New York City. That came about because of a character I had created—a free black midwife. I took a walking tour of New York City, visualizing the old shops and taverns and the faces of people of color—the free Africans and the enslaved ones who were sold at a place called the Meal Market. I stared at the site of the African Burial Ground. I made new trips to the Hudson and even paddled on the Wallkill. The New York of 1760 had seemed like a far-off place, but now it began to seem like right next door.

On the verge of completing *Once on This River,* I met my great-great-aunt Cleopatra Montgomery for the first time. Aunt Cleo's passion turned out to be family genealogy. I had poured a lot of energy into creating the family in *Once on This River.* Thanks to Aunt Cleo's research, I at last had ancestors of my own, with names and occupations and, sometimes, physical descriptions.

Now, when I'm taking a walk along the Hudson, dreaming of the past, I am no longer nagged by that question: Where were the African Americans? They were here! Vital individuals, whose spirits we are now reckoning with.

Acknowledgments

I wish to acknowledge the cooperation and encouragement of the following people and institutions that assisted me during the research phase of *Once on This River*:

Kathleen Johnson, curator, Claudia Dovman, librarian, Ross W. Higgins, and McKelden Smith of Historic Hudson, who welcomed me to Philipsburg and made available the research files pertaining to the African community at the Upper Mills.

Margaret Heilbrun, library director, and the staff of the New-York Historical Society Library for granting permission to quote from documents in the Society's collections.

The staff of the New York Public Library, U.S. Local History and Genealogy Division, as well as the Rare Books and Manuscripts Division and the Office of Special Services for granting permission to quote from original documents.

Staff members of the Schomburg Center for Research in Black Culture in New York City.

The staff of the Office of Public Education and Interpretation of the African Burial Ground.

The staff of the U.S. Customs Service, New York City.

The staff of the Fenimore House Museum in Cooperstown, New York.

The Friends of Historic Kingston, in Kingston, New York.

The Guggenheim Museum for their exhibition "Africa, the Art of a Continent."

Joyce Gold for her walking tour "through history" in downtown New York.

Mr. and Mrs. Peter Johnson and Buz Wyeth, who handed on to me twenty privately owned volumes of "Collections from The New-York Historical Society" from the Johnsons' library.

I am grateful to my friend, midwife Leslie Kotin, for sharing her birthing experiences with me.

I wish to thank Jane Alley for translating my sentiments into the Kuku language for the birth song of the Sudanese women. I met Jane at an African Breakfast at St. Paul's Church in Paterson, New Jersey, where she shared jumqua, a dish made in her native country, Sudan. That same morning, Jane shared the appalling fact that slavery still exists in Sudan today.

Historian Jeanne Chase sent me her research notes for an upcoming book on black life in colonial New York during the eighteenth century; through these writings and conversations with Jeanne, I got my first inkling of the vital African American network in New York during that period, which crisscrossed between free and enslaved people. Jeanne also helped guide me in my own research efforts, steering me to the right books, maps, and places. The scope of Jeanne's knowledge and the intensity of her enthusiasm were of inestimable value to me.

Andrea Cascardi proved a perfect editor. I thank her for her many insights. I am grateful to my publisher, Simon Boughton, for his personal interest and continued support.

My agent, Robin Rue, was, as ever, in my corner. And my friend and consultant Thelma Markowitz listened and responded to every chapter. Mary Pope Osborne continues to be an inspiring force and generous adviser.

Thanks also to my great-great-aunt Cleopatra Montgomery, who told me about the early African Americans in our own family, giving me a greater sense of purpose.

The magic ingredient in all I endeavor is the support of my husband, Sims, and daughter, Georgia.

SOURCE NOTES

CHAPTER ONE: From the account book of the sloop *BV Rhode Island*, Peter James, Master, December 1748–July 1749. [Courtesy of the New-York Historical Society]

CHAPTER TWO: From the petition of Nero Corney, an enslaved African, requesting his freedom, addressed to Attorney General Kemp of New York, circa 1759. New York City Misc. Mss. Box 7, #25. [Courtesy of the New-York Historical Society]

CHAPTER THREE: From the *New York Mercury*, April 16, 1759.

CHAPTER FOUR: From *The Iconography of Manhattan Island, Volume 6: 1498–1909*, by I. N. Phelps Stokes. (New York, 1915; reissued by Arno Press in 1967).

CHAPTER FIVE: From the Adolph Phillipse Inventory, entry dated February 12, 1749. [Courtesy of the Adolph Phillipse Inventory, Manuscripts and Archives Division, the New York Public Library, Astor, Lenox and Tilden Foundations]

CHAPTER SIX: From the *New York Gazette/Weekly Postboy*, April 9, 1750. [Courtesy of the Rare Books Division of the New York Public Library, Astor, Lenox and Tilden Foundations]

CHAPTER SEVEN: Pickled oyster recipe taken from the journal of Peter Kalm, a botanist, *Travels in North America, 1770-1771*.

CHAPTER EIGHT: James Phenix: "Abstracts of Wills on File in the Surrogate's Office, City of New York, vol. V, 1754–1760." *The Collections of The New-York Historical Society for the Year 1896* (New York: The New-York Historical Society, 1897), Liber 22, page 391.

Gerritt Van Bergen: "Abstracts of Wills on File in the Surrogate's Office, City of New York, vol. V, 1754–1760." *The Collections of The New-York Historical Society for the Year 1896* (New York: The New-York Historical Society, 1897), Liber 21, page 325.

Jeremiah Owen: "Abstracts of Wills on File in the Surrogate's Office, City of New York, vol. V, 1754–1760." *The Collections of The New-York Historical Society for the Year 1896* (New York: The New-York Historical Society, 1897), Liber 20, page 112.

CHAPTER NINE: From "Proceedings of the General Court of Assizes," New York, 1680–1682. *The Collections of The New-York Historical Society for the Year 1912* (New York: The New-York Historical Society, 1913), page 34.

CHAPTER TEN: From the *New York Mercury Gazette*, January 15, 1759.

CHAPTER ELEVEN: From the *New York Mercury Gazette*, April 30, 1759.